THE WORLD'S CLASSICS

A MONTH IN THE COUNTRY

IVAN SERGEEVICH TURGENEV (1818–83) was brought up on the estate of his mother at Spasskoe-Lutovinovo and educated at the universities of Moscow and St Petersburg. In 1838 he went to study in Germany and became a convinced believer in the West, or a Westernist (*Zapadnik*). On returning to Russia he gradually turned to literature, first as a poet, then as the author of the famous *Sketches* (*Zapiski okhotnika*, 1847–52), in which he exposed the evils of serfdom. He also began to make a name for himself as a playwright (*A Month in the Country*, 1850), but his life had already become dominated by his devotion to the famous singer, Pauline Viardot. Arrested in 1852 and exiled to Spasskoe, he turned to the larger genre of the short novel, publishing *Rudin* (1856), *Home of the Gentry* (1859), *On the Eve* (1860), and *Fathers and Sons* (1862). The hostile critical reaction to the nihilist hero of this last novel, Bazarov, and his own desire to live close to Pauline Viardot made him choose to live abroad, first in Baden-Baden, then, after the Franco-Prussian War, in Paris. Two further novels (*Smoke*, 1867, and *Virgin Soil*, 1877) followed, in addition to many short stories. By the end of his life his reputation had become overshadowed by his great compatriots, Tolstoy and Dostoevsky, but as the first Russian writer to gain recognition in Europe and America and as a master of the short socio-political novel and the lyrical love story Turgenev still remains matchless among Russian writers.

RICHARD FREEBORN, Emeritus Professor of Russian Literature, University of London, has published several works on Turgenev and the Russian novel. His translations of Turgenev include *First Love and Other Stories* and *Fathers and Sons* in the World's Classics. He is also the author of several novels.

THE WORLD'S CLASSICS

IVAN TURGENEV

A Month in
the Country

Translated and edited by
RICHARD FREEBORN

Oxford   New York
OXFORD UNIVERSITY PRESS
1991

Oxford University Press, Walton Street, Oxford OX2 6DP

Oxford New York Toronto
Delhi Bombay Calcutta Madras Karachi
Petaling Jaya Singapore Hong Kong Tokyo
Nairobi Dar es Salaam Cape Town
Melbourne Auckland

and associated companies in
Berlin Ibadan

Oxford is a trade mark of Oxford University Press

British Library Cataloguing in Publication Data
Data available

Library of Congress Cataloging in Publication Data
Turgenev, Ivan Sergeevich, 1818–1883.
[Mesiats v derevne. English]
A month in the country / Ivan Turgenev ; translated and edited by
Richard Freeborn
p. cm.—(The World's classics)
Translation of: Mesiats v derevne.
Includes bibliographical references.
I. Freeborn, Richard. II. Series.
PG3420.M413 1991 891.73'3—dc20 90-27158
ISBN 0–19–282622–0

Typeset by Cambridge Composing (UK) Ltd
Printed in Great Britain by
BPCC Hazell Books
Aylesbury, Bucks

CONTENTS

INTRODUCTION

As a playwright Turgenev's work was experimental, often derivative and never properly appreciated either by himself or by others in his lifetime. He early began writing for the stage, in the sense that he composed more than one juvenile verse drama, but it was his poetry, especially a long poem entitled *Parasha* (1843), which first brought him critical attention and some modest success. Only later, during the second half of the 1840s and the early 1850s, did he make serious attempts to become a playwright, but he gave up any hope of success in that field after about half a dozen years. At the same time he was enjoying far greater esteem as the author of his famous prose sketches of Russian rural life (*Zapiski okhotnika*), which I have translated as *Sketches from a Hunter's Album*. Later, of course, he was to turn to the form of the short novel, on which his reputation as a writer now principally rests. The realistic social commentary which he offered in his *Sketches* and the theatrical form in which he experimented while writing for the stage were to be combined in his 'month in the country' novels to create harmonious blends of social portraiture and love story, the most remarkable example of which is *Fathers and Sons* (1862).

Turgenev was never a 'dramatic' playwright. He referred to his plays as no more than 'Scenes and Comedies' and his diffidence about them shows itself in the Preface that he wrote to the collection of his *Scenes and Comedies* published in 1869: 'I consider it my duty to explain my motives to my readers. Realizing that I have no dramatic talent, I would not have acceded to the request of my publishers who wished to print the fullest possible edition of my works had I not thought that my plays, although unsatisfactory as pieces for the stage, could be of certain interest as pieces designed for reading.' In his lifetime friends and critics alike generally acquiesced in this view. His was considered to be an intimate theatre, drawing its inspiration very largely from the Parisian theatre of the 1840s. It was only when Stanislavsky brought his subtlety and imagination as a director and actor to a production of *A Month in the Country* in 1909 that this, Turgenev's finest play, was recognized for what it was, a brilliant piece of intimate psychological theatre requiring a company of actors schooled in Stanislavsky's ensemble style to reflect to the full the many nuances in the close weave of the play's emotional texture.

His first play dates from 1843. Entitled *Indiscretion*, it is a curiosity with a Spanish setting, though in its theme of a young wife briefly tempted by the attentions of a young dandy—the momentary 'indiscretion' of the title—it loosely anticipates the theme of *A Month in the Country*. More significantly, there is also a close friend of the husband who reveals that he has long nursed a passion for the wife. In all other respects, the work is melodramatic and uncharacteristic. More relevant to some of Turgenev's later plays is his second work, *A Lack of Money* (written 1845, published 1846) which derives from the vaudevilles fashionable at the time and owes something to the realistic, satirical trend fostered in Russian literature and in the theatre by N. V. Gogol. This short play, with its indictment of the fecklessness of the St Petersburg nobility, is the first 'realistic' work in Turgenev's repertoire and it attracted the hostility of the censorship both when it was first published and more especially when it was first staged, for only two performances, in 1852.

Since neither of these works can be regarded as 'Turgenevan' in spirit, the first of his works for the stage to meet the description adequately was his third play *One May Spin a Thread Too Finely* (1848). It is a witty, ironical piece, based on de Musset's 'theatrical proverbs', with a country house setting and the theme of an 'amorous duel' between a pretty girl and her two suitors, one a staid neighbour and the other a young man who courts the girl more for the fun of the chase than for any serious purpose. Naturally, he finally leaves the field to his rival with greater regret than he had originally anticipated. Elegant and witty dialogue, matched by that acute psychological insight into character which one expects from Turgenev, demonstrated that this style of writing for the stage suited his talent more than the rumbustious, 'Gogolian' form of satirical realism which enjoyed such popularity at the time. But it was this latter form that dictated the style and content of his next three plays.

A Poor Gentleman (1848), *The Bachelor* (1849) and *Lunch with the Marshal of Nobility* (1849) are all comedies containing both an element of social comment, sometimes acute, and something of the grotesque manner which one associates with Gogol. The first play tells of 'a poor gentleman', a hanger-on in a country household, the butt of crude horseplay, who turns out to be the true father of the recently married daughter of the house and thus proves to be too great an embarrassment for all concerned. In two acts, the play was as sharp an indictment of upper-class morals as anything in Turgenev's *Sketches* and its banning by the authorities was hardly surprising. But even when it was finally staged in 1861, only the first act was produced, which meant that it lost much of its critical point.

The Bachelor, written for the famous actor-manager Shchepkin, as had been *A Poor Gentleman*, proved to be Turgenev's only theatrical success. In three acts, it was a contrived and artless work telling of an elderly St Petersburg official who has become a kind of foster-father to an ambitious young man and a young girl. It is his fond hope that they will eventually marry. His plan misfires and it is he, the bachelor, who finally becomes the girl's husband, in anticipation of a similar contrived match in *A Month in the Country* between Verochka and Bolshintsov. The play could boast some amusing scenes and pointed caricatures of officialdom, but the pill of social indictment was too obviously sugared by burlesque comedy for it to have much effect. Although, in the hope of achieving a similar success, a similar burlesque manner was employed to depict the quarrel between two landowners in *Lunch with the Marshal of Nobility*, this short one-act play was instantly banned by the censor.

After *A Month in the Country* Turgenev wrote three plays, of which the most important is the one-act piece *The Provincial Lady* (1850). It describes how the wife of a provincial official exercises her charms on an elderly roué to obtain a position for her husband in St Petersburg. Neatly observed, the piece apparently received rapturous applause when it was first staged in 1851. *Conversation on the High Road* (1851) was virtually little more than a protracted peasant dialogue which made use of several dialect words from Turgenev's native region of Orël. His last play, *An Evening in Sorrento* (1852), was never published during his lifetime. It relates the brief amorous encounters and eventual pairing-off of four Russian tourists on their last evening in Sorrento.

Many critical claims may be made for these early plays, but they have to be regarded as minor and experimental when they are compared with Turgenev's only major work for the theatre, *A Month in the Country* (1848–50). This five-act play has ensured Turgenev an international reputation as a playwright and has become an acknowledged classic of the Russian theatre. Even so, the experimental features of his earlier work—the social element, for instance, of his 'Gogolian' plays and the intimate 'amorous duel' manner of his *One May Spin a Thread Too Finely*—are still clearly discernible. They have combined here in a unique tragi-comic study of the power and absurdity of love in the familiar 'Turgenevan' setting of a Russian country house.

Turgenev may have owed a debt here to Balzac's *La Marâtre*. He was in Paris in April 1848 when Balzac's play had its première and both plays can be shown to have an approximately similar plot involving the rivalry between a young stepmother and her stepdaughter over a young man in the service of the household. The young stepmother decides to marry her adopted daughter off to an obviously unsuitable older man with the help of the local doctor. The plays further resemble each other in being a new kind of intimate theatre. At this point, though, the resemblance largely ceases. Whether or not Turgenev was directly influenced by Balzac's play cannot be ascertained on the available evidence.

In draft form Turgenev gave his play the title *The Student*, which suggests that from the start he was more concerned to emphasize the role of the young student Belyaev than that of the stepmother (Natalya Petrovna) in his comedy. Soviet interpretations have consequently tended to set great store by the social contrasts which arise in the play between the 'classless' Belyaev (a representative of the younger intelligentsia of the time) and the representatives of the landowning nobility. The realistic social reference of the play may therefore be assumed to have had as much importance for Turgenev as the element of amorous duel; but if Turgenev sympathized with the type of Belyaev, he also introduced into his play the figure of Rakitin, the devoted longstanding admirer of the heroine who becomes part-observer and part-victim of the ensuing amorous duel. This creates a dimension entirely absent from Balzac's play. It acknowledges both Turgenev's wish to portray the contrast between two generations of the Russian intelligentsia and the autobiographical fact of the uneasy role which he played personally in his relations with Pauline Viardot in the Viardot household. The fact that Turgenev here reflected his personal dilemma has long been recognized by commentators.

A Month in the Country describes how Natalya Petrovna, loved and admired by her huband Islaev, and her friend of long standing Rakitin, falls in love with Belyaev who has been engaged to teach her son Kolya. The play's title is defined by the fact that Belyaev has been in her employ for approximately a month. Unwittingly a catalyst, the young man simply does not realize until it is already too late how disturbing a presence he has been in the relatively stuffy, isolated world of the Islaev country house. In consequence a number of misunderstandings arise. Natalya Petrovna does not really understand her own feelings, though she is quick enough to take advantage of the local doctor's offer of a husband for her young ward, Verochka, when she comes to realize that the latter is a rival for Belyaev's affections. Her failure of understanding in Verochka's case is matched by Belyaev's failure to understand that either woman is in love with him, just as Islaev, the husband, is somewhat implausibly unaware that Rakitin has been devotedly in love with his wife for four years. When the truth about these emotional relationships becomes known, Rakitin and Belyaev are both obliged to leave. The outcome of this 'month in the country' is that Natalya Petrovna loses both her patient, solicitous admirer of four years' standing and that vision of a younger and perhaps rejuvenating love which she felt Belyaev could offer her.

The play is not a romantic comedy in a conventional sense, although it is about love. The play is labelled a 'comedy' no doubt because it sets out to explore and illumine, in the subtlest and least didactic of ways, the absurdity of human passion. In doing so, of course, it touches upon social differences which are a clue to the play's deeper meaning. Central to this is the young Belyaev. Like the later Bazarov of Turgenev's masterpiece *Fathers and Sons*, for whom he is clearly a trial sketch, Belyaev's social background is uncertain. He is neither of the nobility nor of the peasantry, the principal components of nineteenth-century Russian society. He is therefore 'classless', dissident, dependent like any meritocrat upon his intelligence and education. He is also—to judge from what he says in the play—scornful of poetry and evidently biased towards science. He has a common touch, it seems, which gives him an inherent social mobility, so that he can move with equal ease among children, servants and the landowning nobility.

By contrast, the representative of the supposedly older generation of the intelligentsia (though only nine years in fact separate them), the 'superfluous man' Rakitin, is emotionally old beyond his years. Natalya Petrovna emphasizes this rather callously. In her eyes, Rakitin is unduly 'sensitive', but it is a sensitivity which has a sickliness, a falseness about it that lacks the spontaneous, untutored perception so necessary for a proper understanding of the ways of the heart. When Rakitin, in Act Two, speaks eloquently of the beauty of a dark-green oak, Natalya Petrovna reproves him by saying:

Do you know something, Rakitin? I've been aware of this a long time . . . You have a very delicate feeling for the so-called beauties of nature and you talk about them very elegantly and very cleverly . . . so elegantly and cleverly that I imagine nature must be unspeakably grateful to you for your exquisitely happy expressions of endearment. You run after her like a powdered, perfumed marquis in high-heeled red shoes running after a pretty peasant girl . . . The only thing is I sometimes think that she simply cannot understand and appreciate your sensitive observations, just as a peasant girl wouldn't be able to understand the courtly civilities of a marquis. Nature is much simpler, even cruder, than you suppose, simply because—thank God!—it is healthy . . .

This contrast between nature's healthiness and Rakitin's sensitivity has a social relevance in that it emphasizes the healthy youthfulness of Belyaev as a representative of the younger intelligentsia by contrast with the excessive intro-spection and hypochondria of the older. Natalya Petrovna can easily enough evaluate the relative social merits of the two men. It would be stretching a point to assume that her preference for Belyaev is due to any real acknowledgement of his class difference. She admits he is one of 'them', as it were, and not of her class, even patronizing him in her early relations with him, but by the end of Act Three she has to admit to herself, youthfulness and class difference apart: 'I just grovel before him, he's a real man!' Doubtless, though it is never specified, what she had been seeking all along was 'a real man' to love and be loved by, for her practical, if inarticulate, husband, on the one hand, and her eloquent, long-suffering, rather passive admirer, on the other, could hardly be said to meet the needs of such a wilful, independent-minded and emotionally frustrated woman.

Other social disparities, not immediately evident at the opening of the play, must explain certain features of behaviour in the Islaev household. No doubt the social disparity between Natalya Petrovna and her ward must account in part for her readiness to contemplate such an unequal match as the one between Verochka and Bolshint-sov. Similarly, there is the socially dependent position of the go-between, Dr Shpigelsky. He is simultaneously matchmaker and chorus, a figure whose comments, when they are not directly contributing to the play's comedic element in the frankly burlesque relations with Bolshintsov, have an acerbic and bitter edge to them as a harsh censure of the upper classes. His remarks to Lizaveta Bogdanovna in Act Four endow his role with a critical force that makes him a spokesman for Turgnev's own critical attitude to the mores of the serf-owning nobility.

The social contrasts, then, contribute to the realism of the play as a reflection of its times, but they are for the most part implied rather than overt. They have importance only as reinforcements of the emotional and psychological contrasts which form the weave of the play. At the centre of these is Natalya Petrovna. Her initially unadmitted, but ultimately overwhelming feeling for Belyaev, Rakitin's calm, passive, but unappeasable love for her, her own jealousy of Verochka and her husband's almost inarticulate devotion form the essential emotional patterns which have to be assumed within the play's texture. The audience quickly enough becomes aware of them, though the rele-vance, say, of Natalya Petrovna's fractiousness in Act One or Shpigelsky's anecdote about the girl who could not make up her mind may not be apparent at once. A fact which does not seem to have been given the prominence it deserves is that Rakitin has presumably been absent from the Islaev household for about a month and is only recently returned at the beginning of the play. Otherwise he would presumably have known who Belyaev was and might not, being the sensitive man he is, have been so puzzled by the change in the woman he adores.

In so far as the play takes on the character of an amorous duel, the participants are not evenly matched. Natalya Petrovna has all the advantages at the beginning, as it were, and loses them in the end. Rakitin starts with the disadvantage of being her devoted admirer, the friend enslaved to her affections, and ends by witnessing her

defeat—a defeat which ironically frees him from an enslave-
ment to love that has become, he admits, 'a sickly, consumptive affair'. There is a similar kind of duelling between
Natalya Petrovna, Belyaev and Verochka, in which Natalya
Petrovna ostensibly starts with all the advantages, but
overreaches herself, manipulates Verochka, turns her into
her bitter rival and ends by destroying the likely happiness
of all three participants. Although her desire for love is not
exactly innocent, she is innocent of real malice in her
attempt to gain it. She quickly repents of her plan to match
Verochka with Bolshintsov. Her complex and shifting
motives, like her complex nature, are the result of an
unhappy childhood, as she explains to Belyaev in Act One.
Dominated by an overbearing father who eventually went
blind, she became fearful of him and the resultant embarrassment and shyness remained with her into adulthood.
Her passion for Belyaev seems to spring from a sense of
loss. It is a craving for affection which is part self-
indulgent, part pitiable and part hurtful; but it is also
beyond her control, and in this it seems to be a genuine
and sincere love which has become fixated on Belyaev,
but must be fruitless because the young student, for
reasons of background and character, cannot be expected
to respond to it. The incongruity—and consequent absurdity—of Natalya Petrovna's love for Belyaev is paral-
leled by a similar incongruity in her relations with Rakitin.
She cannot respond to his devoted love in the same way
that Belyaev cannot respond to hers. The emotional needs
of all the play's chief characters remain unfulfilled. As a
study in human incompatibility and its saddening consequences, *A Month in the Country* anticipates Chekhovian
comedy much more obviously than it reflects the comedy of
Gogol.

In contrast to Chekhov's work, Turgenev's play illus-
trates a definable attitude to such a human dilemma. Love,
nature and freedom are the ingredients. As Stanislavsky
pointed out in discussing the play, Natalya Petrovna is
drawn to Belyaev and, for that matter, to Verochka,
because their love is

natural, naïve, simple and, as it were, field-fresh. In seeing these lovers and admiring the simplicity of their relations, Natalya Petrovna is involuntarily drawn to such simple and natural feelings and thus towards nature itself. The hot-house rose sought to become a field flower, started to dream of meadow and woodland: she fell in love with the student Belyaev. From this there came the general catastrophe: Natalya Petrovna frightened away the simple and natural love of Verochka, dismayed the young student, but did not pursue him, was deprived of her faithful admirer Rakitin, remained for ever with a husband whom she could respect but could not love, and retreated once more into her hot-house.

> (K. S. Stanislavsky, *Moya zhizn' v iskusstve*,
> Leningrad–Moscow, 1931, pp. 562–3)

The play can be said to be a study of love in two climates—the climate of the stuffy, restricted, hot-house world in which Natalya Petrovna lives and the field-fresh, 'natural' climate to which Belyaev and Verochka belong. Natalya wanted to free herself from the hot-house world, but was not bold or natural enough to become a dweller for long in the climate of the fields. Rakitin, on the other hand, had no desire to leave the hot-house, but was eventually obliged to choose the freedom of the fields, the greater world outside, after Natalya Petrovna's failure. Love and freedom are here opposed as choices. And what, after all, is love? Rakitin passes a typically Turgenevan verdict on this rather absurd emotion which has been the cause of such happiness and such misery during the course of the comedy. In Act Five, instead of praising love as earth's greatest blessing, he instructs Belyaev in its pitfalls and dangers:

In my opinion, Aleksei Nikolaich, any love, whether happy or unhappy, is a real disaster if you submit to it totally . . . Just hold on a moment! Perhaps you will still get to know how those tender hands can torture, with what gentle solicitude they can tear your heart to shreds . . . Just one moment! You will get to know how much torrid hatred is hidden beneath the most fiery love! You will remember me when, like a sick man yearning for health, you will thirst for peace of mind, the most senseless and most ordinary peace of mind, when you will envy anyone his chance of being unworried and free . . .

The moral of these words, for all their whiff of sour grapes, is that lack of freedom is too high a price to pay. Rakitin accepts with grace that his 'superfluity' in Natalya Petrovna's life, always of course in the offing, has become final, and he therefore gains, one assumes, an unwanted and rather profitless freedom. He has had to choose, as she has, the lesser rather than the greater happiness. These are the contrasts, then, from which the comedy is made: the contrast of youth and age, of one social status with another, of the hot-house climate and the climate of the fields, of love and freedom and the tragic and the comic. Out of such contrasts Turgenev has woven his 'comedy', but it is of course in the words of his laconic, oblique, subtly emotive dialogue that the true appeal of his masterpiece resides. This is where the words of Toby Robertson, who had experience of producing the play, have a telling aptness:

The key to *A Month in the Country* lies in its sharp-witted, highly concentrated, bitingly passionate text, a text which yields surprising comedy. Yet, if Turgenev's intention is to show the absurdity of romantic love, however comic the effect, the truth of the underlying passion can never be forgotten. It is a wonderful tightrope for any actor and a challenge to any translator. The exactness of a phrase is all.

(Introduction to *A Month in the Country*, tr. A. Nicolaeff, London, 1976)

The most stout-hearted of translators must blench at such a thought, this one no less than others. The exactness of phrase is, of course, essential, but it must also be said that it is a mid-nineteenth-century exactness which, for all its durable quality, has a pervasively literary, even a faintly salon air to it. A translator must acknowledge this quality in it as much as the limpid and simple directness of the Russian. Largely, one imagines, because he never enjoyed the laboratory experience of close connection with a play's production, Turgenev liked to insist that his play was 'not really a comedy, but a short story in dramatic form' and went on to claim that 'it is clearly not suitable for the stage.' He made such a negative pronouncement when the

play was first published in 1855 and it is readily understandable in the light of the treatment meted out by the
censors.

Entitled *Two Women* when first submitted for publication
in November 1850, it was immediately banned. Despite
this, it enjoyed considerable success in St Petersburg salons
during the autumn of that year. But when Turgenev tried
to publish it in 1855 in *The Contemporary* under its new and
final title *A Month in the Country*, he was obliged by the
censor to cut out the figure of Islaev and to make Natalya
Petrovna into a widow. In the censor's eyes, a married
woman should not be shown entertaining lovers; other cuts
toned down the socio-political significance of Belyaev, the
sharpness of Shpigelsky's comments and Rakitin's bitter
tirade against love. It was not until almost twenty years
after it was completed that the play was published in an
'authorized' version. By this time, in 1869, Turgenev had
already made his reputation as a novelist and few people
remembered that he had earlier been a dramatist. His
insistence that he had no dramatic talent and that his plays
were to be read rather than acted did not help.

During the 1870s the play received its first public performances, firstly—and unsuccessfully—in January 1872,
and secondly—this time with real success—in 1879 when
it was produced at the Alexandrinsky Theatre in St Petersburg by the young actress Savina. She took the part of
Verochka. Turgenev was delighted by her performance and
fell in love with her. Critical reactions to the play were
mixed, but audiences seem to have enjoyed the merits of
this half-forgotten and long-unrecognized comedy when it
finally received a sympathetic production.

True and lasting success came to this play only many
years after Turgenev's death. The association of the work
with Chekhovian comedy has become a commonplace of
criticism, though it is very likely that in terms of theatrical
history Turgenev's work should be regarded paradoxically
as owing more to Chekhov's influence than exerting any
prior influence of its own. The success of Chekhov's plays
in the first years of the twentieth century was to provide

the kind of theatrical atmosphere in which an intimate, psychological comedy like *A Month in the Country* could be properly appreciated. Stanislavsky recognized this. He was particularly sensitive to the extremely delicate skeins of amorous experience which form the weave of Turgenev's comedy. He felt that his own acting method could be applied successfully to the role of Rakitin (the part which he played in the famous 1909 production at the Moscow Art Theatre) and to the other roles. He believed that a special kind of acting was required 'which would allow the theatre-goer to appreciate the delicate psychological patterns made by the loving, suffering, envying hearts' of the play's characters. 'Let the actors sit motionless and feel and talk and infect thus the thousandfold audience with their experiences. Let there be no more than a garden bench or a divan on the stage, on which all the characters sit, so that everyone can see the unfolding of the inner essence of their souls and Turgenev's complex picture of psychological interrelationships . . .' (op. cit. 563–4). In this way the inner picture of *A Month in the Country* would be revealed and the actor's concern would be to reveal the spiritual activity defined by the psychological picture of his role.

The play, of course, is long. A producer or director will be bound to make cuts. The use of soliloquy presupposes both an old-fashioned style and a commonsense recognition that people *do* talk to themselves. Much of the dialogue, especially in its confessional character, invites an abandonment of reticence, a thinning or expunging of the line between the public *persona* and the private person. These are difficult and challenging features of a 'comedy' that presents a number of multifaceted roles for a cast of actors and actresses of varying ages and range. The balance, though, between the comedic and serious or potentially tragic aspects of the work must depend to a great extent on the playing of the central role of Natalya Petrovna. The self-deluding, passionate, manipulative facets of her character have to be reined in by an awareness of the manifest honesty with which she confronts her own weaknesses, a process continuously watched over with a special degree of

0 xx INTRODUCTION

loving fondness by Rakitin and with lesser degrees of
sympathy and understanding by her husband and other
members of the household.

The special charm of the work lies not in its Russian-
ness, nor in its nineteenth-century quality—it is, in fact,
surprisingly modern—but in its exploration of what lies
beneath the ephemeral nature of relationships and hopes
and supposed certainties. Belyaev, in saying goodbye to
Verochka in Act Five, somewhat dismissively remarks of
all the emotional involvements of the three days or so of the
play's action that 'everything ... flared up and went out
like a spark.' It succinctly enough summarizes the rapid
way in which love can be said to have come and gone in
the play. Poignantly, beneath the ephemeral surface of
events, a tragic comedy of human incompatibility, inadequacy and heartbreak has been played out, dependent
throughout on the buoyancy of the language, its many
shades of humour ranging from the sophisticated to the
satirical and its gentle eloquence embracing the everyday,
conversational manner of a leisured class, the common
speech of servants, the inarticulacy of high passion and
those golden strands of Turgenevan poetry which finally
unite it.

In conclusion, I should like to acknowledge the enormous
help I have received from Virginia Llewellyn Smith, without whose careful and sensitive contribution as editor this
translation would be far less accurate and readable.

R. F.

SELECT BIBLIOGRAPHY

1. ENGLISH TRANSLATIONS

Only two full translations of Turgenev's comedy are readily available in English, those by Constance Garnett and Sir Isaiah Berlin. There have been several versions or adaptations. Noteworthy, though now dated, is the adaptation by Emlyn Williams, with an introduction by Michael Redgrave (London, 1943, 1981). The translation by Ariadne Nicolaeff (London, 1976), with an introduction by Toby Robertson, is a shortened and altered version of the original text.

2. CRITICISM

Critical materials on the play are scanty. Some of the more recent and valuable examples are given below (in chronological order).

Sir Isaiah Berlin, Introductory Note to his translation of *A Month in the Country* (London, 1981)

Nick Worrall, *Nikolai Gogol and Ivan Turgenev* (London, 1982)

Richard Freeborn, 'Turgenev, the Dramatist', *Transactions of the Association of Russian-American Scholars in the USA*, vol. 16 (New York, 1983), pp. 57–74

Walter Koschmal, *Das poetische System der Dramen I. S. Turgenevs* (Munich, 1983)

A. V. Knowles, *Ivan Turgenev*, Twayne World Authors (Boston, 1988), pp. 19–25

A CHRONOLOGY OF
IVAN TURGENEV

1818   28 October: born in Orël, Russia, second son of
            Varvara Petrovna T. (*née* Lutovinova), six years
            older—and considerably wealthier—than Sergei Niko-
            laevich, his father.

1822–3   Turgenev family makes European tour. Ivan rescued
            from bear pit in Bern by his father.

1833   Enters Moscow University after summer spent in
            dacha near Moscow which provided the setting for his
            story 'First love' (1860).

1834   Transfers to St Petersburg University. 30 October:
            father dies.

1838–41   Studies at Berlin University and travels in Germany
            and Italy. Friendships with Granovsky, Stankevich,
            Herzen and Bakunin.

1842   26 April: birth of illegitimate daughter. Writes master's
            dissertation, but fails to obtain professorship at St
            Petersburg University.

1843   Enters Ministry of Interior. Meets Belinsky. Long
            poem *Parasha* brings him literary fame. Meets Pauline
            Viardot.

1844   'Andrei Kolosov', first published short story.

1845   Resigns from Ministry of Interior. Meets Dostoevsky.

1847   First of *Sketches from a Hunter's Album* 'Khor and Kali-
            nych' published in newly revived journal *The
            Contemporary*.

1847–50   Lives in Paris or at Courtavenel, country house of the
            Viardots.

1850   'The Diary of a Superfluous Man'. Completes only
            major play, *A Month in the Country*. 16 November:
            mother dies. Inherits family estate of Spasskoe-
            Lutovinovo.

1852   *Sketches* published in separate edition. 16 April: arrested for obituary on Gogol, but really for publication of *Sketches*. Imprisoned for one month. Exiled to Spasskoe till November 1853.

1855   Meets Tolstoy.

1856   *Rudin*, first novel, published in *The Contemporary*. Travels widely, visiting Berlin, London and Paris. Till 1862 is abroad each summer.

1859   *Home of the Gentry*.

1860   *On the Eve*. 'First Love.' 12 August–2 September: Ventnor, Isle of Wight, and Bournemouth. Conceives figure of Bazarov.

1861   14 February: Emancipation of the serfs. Quarrels with Tolstoy, leading to a 17-year estrangement.

1862   *Fathers and Sons*.

1863   Beginning of his 'absenteeism' from Russia. Takes up permanent residence in Baden-Baden, close to Viardots.

1867   *Smoke*. Quarrels with Dostoevsky.

1870   'King Lear of the Steppes.' Resides for a time in London, driven from Baden-Baden by Franco-Prussian War.

1871   Moves to Paris, residing mostly at Bougival. Flaubert, George Sand, Zola, Daudet, Edmond de Goncourt and Henry James among his friends.

1872   'Torrents of Spring.'

1877   *Virgin Soil*.

1878   Reconciliation with Tolstoy.

1879   Received in triumph on visit to Russia. 18 June: awarded honorary doctorate of civil law by University of Oxford.

1880   7 June: at celebrations to mark the unveiling of the Pushkin monument in Moscow, Turgenev's speech greeted coolly. 8 June: famous speech by Dostoevsky leads to public reconciliation between the writers.

1883   3 September: dies at Bougival from mis-diagnosed cancer of the spine after long illness. 27 September: buried at Volkovo cemetery in St Petersburg.

A MONTH IN THE COUNTRY

Dramatis personae

ARKADY SERGEICH ISLAEV, a rich landowner, 36

NATALYA PETROVNA, his wife, 29

KOLYA, their son, 10

VEROCHKA, a ward, 17

ANNA SEMËNOVNA (*pronounced* Semyonovna) ISLAEVA, Islaev's mother, 58

LIZAVETA BOGDANOVNA, a lady companion, 37

SCHAAF. a German tutor, 45

MIKHAILO ALEKSANDROVICH RAKITIN, a friend of the family, 30

ALEKSEI NIKOLAEVICH BELYAEV, a student, Kolya's teacher, 21

AFANASY IVANOVICH BOLSHINTSOV, a neighbour, 48

IGNATY ILICH SHPIGELSKY, a doctor, 40

MATVEI, a servant, 40

KATYA, a maid, 20

The action occurs on the Islaev estate, at the beginning of the 1840s. Between Acts One and Two, Two and Three and Four and Five there is an interval of one day in each case.*

ACT ONE

*The scene is a drawing-room. To the right are a card table and
the door to the study; straight ahead is the door into the hall;
to the left are two windows and a round table. There are divans
in the corners.* ANNA SEMËNOVNA, LIZAVETA BOGDA-
NOVNA, *and* SCHAAF *are seated at the card table playing*
préférence;* NATALYA PETROVNA *and* RAKITIN *are
seated at the round table.* NATALYA PETROVNA *is embroi-
dering on a canvas,* RAKITIN *has a book in his hands. A wall
clock shows three o'clock.*

SCHAAF. Hearts.

ANNA SEMËNOVNA. Again? My good sir, you'll quite wear
us out the way you're going.

SCHAAF [*phlegmatically*]. Eight of hearts.

ANNA SEMËNOVNA [*to Lizaveta Bogdanovna*]. What a man!
It's impossible to play with him. [*Lizaveta Bogdanovna
smiles.*]

NATALYA PETROVNA [*to Rakitin*]. Why have you stopped?
Please go on reading.

RAKITIN [*slowly raising the book*]. 'Monte-Cristo se redressa
haletant . . .'* Natalya Petrovna, does this interest you?

NATALYA PETROVNA. Not in the least.

RAKITIN. Then why are we reading it?

NATALYA PETROVNA. I'll tell you why. Recently a lady
said to me: "You haven't read *Monte-Cristo*? Then you
must, it's a delight." I didn't say anything to her then,
but now I can tell her I've read it and I didn't find
anything delightful in it at all.

RAKITIN. Well, now if you've already managed to convince
yourself . . .

NATALYA PETROVNA. Oh, what a lazybones you are!

RAKITIN. Good heavens, I'm quite ready to go on . . . [*Finding the place where he had stopped*.] '*Se redressa haletant, et . . .*'

NATALYA PETROVNA [*interrupting him*]. Have you seen Arkady this morning?

RAKITIN. I came across him on the dam . . . It's being repaired. He was explaining something to the workers and, to make his point clearer, he waded into the sand up to his knees.

NATALYA PETROVNA. He undertakes everything with far too much zeal . . . he tries too hard. That's a drawback. Don't you think so?

RAKITIN. I agree with you.

NATALYA PETROVNA. How boring! . . . You always agree with me. Please go on reading.

RAKITIN. Ah, I see! You'd like me to argue with you . . . Certainly.

NATALYA PETROVNA. I'd like . . . I'd like . . . I'd like it if *you'd* like . . . Please go on reading, that's an order.

RAKITIN. Madame, I obey. [*He picks up the book again*.]

SCHAAF. Hearts.

ANNA SEMËNOVNA. What, again? This is intolerable! [*To Natalya Petrovna*.] Natasha . . . Natasha . . .

NATALYA PETROVNA. What?

ANNA SEMËNOVNA. Just imagine, Schaaf has quite worn us out . . . all the time seven and eight, always in hearts.

SCHAAF. Right now ist seven.

ANNA SEMËNOVNA. Do you hear that? It's dreadful.

NATALYA PETROVNA. Yes . . . dreadful.

ANNA SEMËNOVNA. That's whist for you! [*To Natalya Petrovna*.] Where's Kolya?

NATALYA PETROVNA. He went for a walk with the new tutor.

ANNA SEMËNOVNA. Ah! Lizaveta Bogdanovna, I invite you to start.

RAKITIN [*to Natalya Petrovna*]. What tutor is that?

NATALYA PETROVNA. Oh, yes! I'd forgotten to tell you . . . when you weren't here we hired a new tutor.

RAKITIN. In place of Dufour?

NATALYA PETROVNA. No . . . a Russian tutor. The princess will be sending us a Frenchman from Moscow.

RAKITIN. What sort of a person is he, this Russian? Old?

NATALYA PETROVNA. No, young. Still, we've only taken him for the summer months.

RAKITIN. Ah, it's a vacation job!

NATALYA PETROVNA. Yes, it seems that's what it's called. And do you know something, Rakitin? You're very fond of observing people, analysing them, poking about inside them . . .

RAKITIN. For heaven's sake, what on earth makes you . . .

NATALYA PETROVNA. Well, you are, you know . . . Just you turn your attention to him. He appeals to me. He's thin, well-built, has a happy look in his eyes and a bold expression . . . You'll see. True, he's a bit graceless . . . and for you that's a very bad thing.

RAKITIN. Natalya Petrovna, you're being dreadfully hard on me today.

NATALYA PETROVNA. Joking apart, just you concentrate on him. I think he could turn out to be really splendid. Still, there's no knowing!

RAKITIN. You rouse my curiosity . . .

NATALYA PETROVNA. Do I? [*Thoughtfully.*] Please go on reading.

RAKITIN. '*Se redressa haletant, et . . .*'

NATALYA PETROVNA [*suddenly looking round her*]. Where's Vera? I haven't seen her since this morning. [*With a smile towards Rakitin.*] Don't bother with that book. I can see you'll have no success with your reading today . . . It'd be better if you told me something . . .

RAKITIN. Certainly . . . Now what have I got to tell you? Well, you know I've been spending some days with the Krinitsyns . . . Just imagine, those young people are already getting bored.

NATALYA PETROVNA. What made you notice that?

RAKITIN. Do you think you can hide boredom. Everything else can be hidden, but not boredom.

NATALYA PETROVNA [giving him a look]. Everything else?

RAKITIN [after a short pause]. I think so.

NATALYA PETROVNA [lowering her eyes]. So what did you do at the Krinitsyns?

RAKITIN. Nothing. Being bored while with one's friends is a dreadful thing—you feel perfectly at home, you're completely relaxed, you're fond of them, you've got nothing to be nasty about, but boredom still drives you frantic and your heart pines and pines as if it were starved to death.

NATALYA PETROVNA. You must be often bored when with your friends.

RAKITIN. As if you didn't know what it's like to have constantly with you someone whom you love and who bores you stiff!

NATALYA PETROVNA [slowly]. Whom you love . . . that's a strong word. You have an odd way of putting things.

RAKITIN. Odd . . . why odd?

NATALYA PETROVNA. Yes, that's your problem. Do you know something, Rakitin: You're, of course, very clever, but . . . [She pauses.]. . . sometimes when we're discussing things it's just as if we were making lace . . . Have you seen how they make lace? In stuffy rooms, always sitting still . . . Lace is beautiful, but a glass of cold water on a hot day is very much better.

RAKITIN. Natalya Petrovna, today you're . . .

NATALYA PETROVNA. What?

RAKITIN. You're angry with me for some reason today.

NATALYA PETROVNA. Oh, you sensitive people, how lacking in perception you are although you're sensitive! No, I'm not angry with you.

ANNA SEMËNOVNA. Ah, at last he's in a mess! He's done for! [*To Natalya Petrovna.*] Natasha, our villain's in a mess!

SCHAAF [*sourly*]. Eet ist all fault of Lisafet Bogdanovna . . .

LIZAVETA BOGDANOVNA [*heatedly*]. Forgive me, sir, I couldn't know Anna Semënovna had no hearts.

SCHAAF. In future I not invite Lisafet Bogdanovna.

ANNA SEMËNOVNA [*to Schaaf*]. What on earth's she done wrong?

SCHAAF [*repeating in the very same voice*]. In future I not invite Lisafet Bogdanovna.

LIZAVETA BOGDANOVNA. Well I never! Just listen to him!

RAKITIN. The more I look at you, Natalya Petrovna, the less I recognize you today.

NATALYA PETROVNA [*with some curiosity*]. Is that so?

RAKITIN. Really and truly. I find there has been some change in you.

NATALYA PETROVNA. You do? In that case, do me a favour . . . You know me, after all—have a guess what this change is that has taken place in me—eh?

RAKITIN. Just a moment . . . [*Kolya suddenly runs noisily into the room from the hall straight to Anna Semënovna.*]

KOLYA. Granny, Granny, look what I've got! [*Shows her a bow and arrows.*] Look!

ANNA SEMËNOVNA. Show me, my dear . . . Oh, what a splendid bow! Who made it for you?

KOLYA. He did . . . he did . . . [*He points to Belyaev who has stopped in the hall doorway.*]

ANNA SEMËNOVNA. Oh, it's so well made . . .

KOLYA. I've already shot at a tree with it, Granny, and hit it twice. [*He jumps with joy.*]

NATALYA PETROVNA. Show me, Kolya.

KOLYA [*runs to her, while Natalya Petrovna looks at the bow*]. Oh, Mummy, Aleksei Nikolaich is so good at climbing trees! He wants to teach me how to, and he also wants to teach me how to swim. He'll teach me everything, everything! [*He jumps about.*]

NATALYA PETROVNA [*to Belyaev*]. I am very grateful to you for taking such trouble with Kolya . . .

KOLYA [*interrupting her in his excitement*]. I like him very much, *Maman*, very much indeed!

NATALYA PETROVNA [*stroking Kolya's head*]. Being with me, he's grown into a bit of a softy . . . Please turn him into an active, athletic boy for me. [*Belyaev bows.*]

KOLYA. Aleksei Nikolaich, let's go to the stables, we'll take Favourite some bread.

BELYAEV. Let's go.

ANNA SEMËNOVNA [*to Kolya*]. Come here, give me a kiss first . . .

KOLYA [*running away*]. Later, Granny, later! [*Runs out into the hall. Belyaev goes after him.*]

ANNA SEMËNOVNA [*watching Kolya go*]. What a charming boy! [*To Schaaf and Lizaveta Bogdanovna.*] Don't you think so?

LIZAVETA BOGDANOVNA. Of course he is, ma'am.

SCHAAF [*after a moment's pause*]. I pass.

NATALYA PETROVNA [*with a certain liveliness to Rakitin*]. Well, how did he strike you?

RAKITIN. Who?

NATALYA PETROVNA [*after a pause*]. The . . . the Russian tutor.

RAKITIN. Ah, forgive me—it had slipped my mind . . . I was so preoccupied by the question you had put to me . . .

[*Natalya Petrovna looks at him with a scarcely discernible grin.*] Anyhow his face is . . . actually it's . . . yes, he has a nice face. I like him. Except he seems to be very shy.

NATALYA PETROVNA. Yes.

RAKITIN [*looking at her*]. But still I can't be sure . . .

NATALYA PETROVNA. What would you say to us concerning ourselves with his education, Rakitin? Would you like that? Let's be a finishing school for him. It's a splendid opportunity for upright, sensible people like ourselves! We are very sensible people, aren't we?

RAKITIN. The young man has taken your fancy. If he knew that . . . he'd be very flattered.

NATALYA PETROVNA. Oh, believe me, that's simply not true! One has no way of telling what . . . what people like us would do in his place. After all, he's not in the least like us, Rakitin. It's our great drawback, my friend, that we study ourselves very assiduously and afterwards imagine we know other people.

RAKITIN. Another's soul is a dark forest, as they say. But what are you dropping all these hints for? Why do you taunt me all the time?

NATALYA PETROVNA. Who should one taunt if not one's friends? And you're my friend, you know that. [*She presses his hand. Rakitin smiles and brightens.*] You're my friend of long standing.

RAKITIN. I'm simply frightened . . . that this friend of long standing might have begun to bore you . . .

NATALYA PETROVNA [*laughing*]. It's only nice things that grow boring.

RAKITIN. Perhaps . . . Only that doesn't make it any easier for them.

NATALYA PETROVNA. Enough's enough . . . [*Lowering her voice.*] As if you didn't know . . . *ce que vous êtes pour moi.**

RAKITIN. Natalya Petrovna, you're playing with me like a cat with a mouse . . . but the mouse isn't complaining.

NATALYA PETROVNA. Oh, you poor little mouse, you!

ANNA SEMËNOVNA. That's twenty you owe me, Adam Ivanych . . . Aha!

SCHAAF. In future I not invite Lisafet Bogdanovna.

MATVEI [entering from the hall and announcing]. Ignaty Ilich has arrived, ma'am.

SHPIGELSKY [entering on his heels]. Doctors are never announced. [Matvei leaves.] My most humble respects to the entire family. [Approaches Anna Semënovna and kisses her hand.] How do you do, my good lady? Do I take it you are winning?

ANNA SEMËNOVNA. Winning! I've only just recouped my losses—and that only by the grace of God! It's all this rogue's doing. [Pointing at Schaaf.]

SHPIGELSKY [to Schaaf]. Adam Ivanych, such conduct with the ladies! That is not nice. I can't think what's come over you.

SCHAAF [growling through his teeth]. Viz ze ladies, viz ze ladies . . .

SHPIGELSKY [approaching the round table on the left]. How do you do, Natalya Petrovna! How do you do, Mikhailo Aleksandrych!

NATALYA PETROVNA. Good afternoon, doctor. How are you today?

SHPIGELSKY. I like being asked that question very much. It means that you are well. How am I today? A decent doctor never suffers from ill health. He just suddenly ups and dies . . . Ha-ha!

NATALYA PETROVNA. Do sit down. I am well, it is true . . . but I'm not in good spirits, and that's surely also a sign of bad health.

SHPIGELSKY [sitting down beside Natalya Petrovna]. Allow me to feel your pulse. [He feels her pulse.] Oh, nerves, nerves, all this nerviness . . . You take too little exercise, Natalya Petrovna . . . You laugh too little . . . That's what's wrong . . . Mikhailo Aleksandrych, why are you looking like that? However, I can prescribe some white drops.

NATALYA PETROVNA. I have nothing against laughing . . . [*With animation.*] Take yourself, doctor, you're a man with a malicious tongue. I love you very much for that and I respect you, granted. So tell me something amusing. Mikhailo Aleksandrych can do nothing but philosophize today.

SHPIGELSKY [*giving Rakitin a sidelong glance*]. Ah, evidently, it's not just a case of nerves, there's a spot of peevishness as well . . .

NATALYA PETROVNA. Well, there you go again! Please diagnose as much as you like, doctor, but not aloud. We all know you're frightfully perceptive . . . You're both very perceptive men.

SHPIGELSKY. At your service, ma'am.

NATALYA PETROVNA. Tell us something amusing.

SHPIGELSKY. Your wish is my command. But I didn't come prepared, didn't guess it'd be a case of 'a flick of the fingers, you there, tell me something.' Permit me to take a pinch of snuff. [*Sniffs.*]

NATALYA PETROVNA. Such lengthy preparations!

SHPIGELSKY. My dear Natalya Petrovna, you must, after all, bear in mind that there is humour and there is humour. It depends on who is being told what. Your neighbour, Mr Khlopushkin, for instance, only needs to be shown a finger stuck up like that and he goes off into a torrent of laughter and wheezes and sheds tears . . . But you, after all . . . However, permit me. Do you know Verenitsyn, Platon Vasilevich?

NATALYA PETROVNA. I think I know him or I've heard of him.

SHPIGELSKY. He has a sister who is quite mad. To my way of thinking, they're either both mad or both completely sane because there's not a scrap of difference whatever between brother and sister, but that's neither here nor there. Fate, ma'am, fate is everywhere at work, fate, ma'am, is what it's all about. Verenitsyn has a daughter, a pale greenish little thing, you know what I mean, with pale little eyes and a small reddish nose and yellowish little teeth—well, in short, a very attractive girl. She can play the piano and speaks with a lisp, so everything's just as it should be. She has two hundred serfs and her aunt's got another hundred and fifty. Her aunt's still alive and will go on living for ever and ever, because all mad people live for ever and ever—after all, there's got to be some compensation for the afflictions in this life! She has made a will in her niece's favour, and only the day before she did so I used my own fair hands to pour a bucket of water over her head—and quite pointlessly, besides, because there's not the slightest chance of curing her. Well, as it's turned out, Verenitsyn has a daughter who is eminently marriageable. He began taking her out to parties and suitors began appearing, among them a certain Perekuzov, an insipid young man, diffident, but with excellent credentials. So you see, the father liked Perekuzov, and so did the daughter—it would seem, wouldn't it, that that was that and, God willing, they'd be married! And in fact everything went along swimmingly. Mr Verenitsyn, Platon Vasilich, had already begun familiarly poking Mr Perekuzov in the tummy—you know what I mean—and slapping him on the shoulder, when suddenly, out of nowhere, an officer drops by, Ardalion Protobekasov! At a ball given by the marshal of nobility he caught sight of Verenitsyn's daughter, danced three polkas with her, no doubt said to her rolling up his eyes: 'Oh, how miserable I am!'—and my young lady's fallen for him hook, line and sinker. There follow tears and sighs and oh's and ah's ... Perekuzov's out of the picture, she won't talk to him, the very word 'marriage' makes her writhe in torment ... My God, what a state of things, believe you me! Well, thinks Verenitsyn, if it's Protobekasov, let it be Protobekasov. Thank heavens he's also a man of some substance. Protobekasov is invited to pay his respects. He pays his

respects—pays his visits, does his courting, falls in love
and finally offers his hand and heart. What would you
think now? The Verenitsyn girl would instantly consent
with pleasure, eh? Not at all! God preserve us! Once
more tears, sighs and fainting fits. The father doesn't
know where to turn. 'What is it? What's the matter?' he
asks her. And what do you think she replies? 'I don't
know which I love, Daddy, the one or the other.' '*What?*'
'Daddy, I really don't know and it's better if I don't
marry either of them, though I love them both!' Verenitsyn, it goes without saying, flies off the handle and the
suitors also have no idea where they stand. But she sticks
to what she's said. So you can judge for yourself, ma'am,
what wonders there are occurring among us!

NATALYA PETROVNA. I don't find anything surprising in
it at all ... Do you think it's impossible to love two
people at the same time?

RAKITIN. Ah! You think you can.

NATALYA PETROVNA [*slowly*]. I think I can ... Still, I
don't know. Perhaps it simply proves you're not in love
with either of them.

SHPIGELSKY [*taking snuff and glancing alternately at Natalya
Petrovna and Rakitin*]. So that's it, that's it ...

NATALYA PETROVNA [*vivaciously to Shpigelsky*]. Your story
was very good, but you still haven't made me laugh.

SHPIGELSKY. My dear lady, who indeed can make you
laugh now? That's not what you need now.

NATALYA PETROVNA. What do I need?

SHPIGELSKY [*with a look of pretend humility*]. God alone
knows.

NATALYA PETROVNA. Oh, what a bore you are, no better
than Rakitin.

SHPIGELSKY. No offence intended, I assure you ...

[*Natalya Petrovna makes an impatient gesture.*]

ANNA SEMËNOVNA [*rising*]. Well, at last ... [*She gives a*

sigh.] My feet have quite gone to sleep. [*Lizaveta Bogdanovna and Schaaf also rise.*] O-o-oh.

NATALYA PETROVNA [*rising and going to them*]. Fancy
spending so long sitting down . . . [*Shpigelsky and Rakitin
rise.*]

ANNA SEMËNOVNA [*to Schaaf*]. You owe me seventy
kopecks, my good sir. [*Schaaf bows drily.*] You can't get
the better of us all the time. [*To Natalya Petrovna.*] You
look a bit pale today, Natasha. Are you feeling well?
Shpigelsky, is she well?

SHPIGELSKY [*who is whispering something to Rakitin*]. Oh,
perfectly well!

ANNA SEMËNOVNA. So that's all right . . . I'll go and have
a little lie-down before dinner . . . I'm tired out. Liza,
let's go . . . oh, my feet, my feet . . . [*She goes into the hall
in the company of Lizaveta Bogdanovna. Natalya Petrovna
accompanies her to the door. Shpigelsky, Rakitin and Schaaf
remain downstage.*]

SHPIGELSKY [*to Schaaf, offering him snuff*]. Well, Adam
Ivanych, *wie befinden Sie sich?*

SCHAAF [*sniffing solemnly*]. Kvite good. End how ar-re you?

SHPIGELSKY. My humble thanks, I am getting by. [*To
Rakitin in a low voice.*] So you really have no idea what's
wrong with Natalya Petrovna today?

RAKITIN. Really and truly, I don't know.

SHPIGELSKY. Well, if *you* don't know . . . [*Turns and goes to
meet Natalya Petrovna who is returning from the door.*] I have a
little matter to discuss with you, Natalya Petrovna.

NATALYA PETROVNA [*going to the window*]. Really, what
is it?

SHPIGELSKY. I have to speak to you alone . . .

NATALYA PETROVNA. Heavens—you quite frighten me.
[*Meanwhile, Rakitin has taken Schaaf by the arm and is walking
to and fro with him, whispering in his ear in German. Schaaf
laughs and says in a low voice: 'Ja, ja, ja, jawohl, jawohl, sehr
gut.'*]

SHPIGELSKY [*in a low voice*]. The matter doesn't only concern you personally . . .

NATALYA PETROVNA [*looking out into the garden*]. What do you mean?

SHPIGELSKY. It's like this, ma'am. A good friend of mine has asked me to discover—er, so to speak—your intentions regarding your ward—Vera Aleksandrovna.

NATALYA PETROVNA. My intentions?

SHPIGELSKY. That's to say—without mincing matters, my friend . . .

NATALYA PETROVNA. He's not surely offering his hand in marriage, is he?

SHPIGELSKY. Precisely, ma'am.

NATALYA PETROVNA. You must be joking?

SHPIGELSKY. Not in the least, ma'am.

NATALYA PETROVNA [*laughing*]. She's still a child, for heaven's sake! What an extraordinary errand you've undertaken!

SHPIGELSKY. Why extraordinary, Natalya Petrovna? My friend . . .

NATALYA PETROVNA. You're a great one for wheeling and dealing, Shpigelsky . . . Who is your friend?

SHPIGELSKY [*smiling*]. Allow me, please . . . You've not said to me anything positive yet regarding . . .

NATALYA PETROVNA. That's enough, doctor. Vera is still a child. You know that yourself, Mr Diplomat. [*Turning round.*] Besides, here she is. [*Vera and Kolya dash in from the hall.*]

KOLYA [*running up to Rakitin*]. Rakitin, tell them to let us have some glue, some glue . . .

NATALYA PETROVNA [*to Vera*]. Where've you come from? [*Strokes her on the cheek.*] How flushed you are . . .

VERA. From the garden . . . [*Shpigelsky bows to her.*] How do you do, Ignaty Ilich.

RAKITIN [*to Kolya*]. What do you want glue for?

KOLYA. We must have it, we must . . . Aleksei Nikolaich is making a kite for us . . . Tell them . . .

RAKITIN [*about to ring*]. Just a moment, in a minute . . .

SCHAAF. Erlauben Sie . . . Mistah Kolya zis morgen his schulebook ist not reating . . . [*Takes Kolya by the hand.*] Kommen Sie.

KOLYA [*crestfallen*]. Morgen, Herr Schaaf, morgen . . .

SCHAAF [*sharply*]. *Morgen, morgen, nur nicht heute, sagen alle faule Leute** . . . Kommen Sie . . . [*Kolya digs his heels in.*]

NATALYA PETROVNA [*to Vera*]. Who have you been out with for so long? I haven't seen you since this morning.

VERA. With Aleksei Nikolaich . . . and with Kolya . . .

NATALYA PETROVNA. Ah! [*Turning round.*] Kolya, what's the meaning of this?

KOLYA [*in a low voice*]. Mr Schaaf, Mummy . . .

RAKITIN [*to Natalya Petrovna*]. Out there they are making kites, but in here they want to give him a lesson.

SCHAAF [*on his dignity*]. *Gnädige Frau* . . .

NATALYA PETROVNA [*sternly, to Kolya*]. Please do what you're told, you've done enough running about for today. Go off with Mr Schaaf.

SCHAAF [*taking Kolya into the hall*]. *Es ist unerhört!**

KOLYA [*whispering to Rakitin as he goes out*]. You'll tell them to get some glue, won't you . . . [*Rakitin nods.*]

SCHAAF [*pulling Kolya*]. *Kommen Sie, mein Herr* . . .

　　[*He goes out with him into the hall. Rakitin goes out after them.*]

NATALYA PETROVNA [*to Vera*]. Sit down . . . You must be tired. [*Sits down herself.*]

VERA [*sitting down*]. Not at all, ma'am.

NATALYA PETROVNA [*smiling at Shpigelsky*]. Shpigelsky, look at her, doesn't she look tired?

SHPIGELSKY. I think it suits Vera Aleksandrovna well.

NATALYA PETROVNA. I wasn't talking about . . . [*To Vera.*] Well, what have you been doing in the garden?

VERA. We've been playing games, ma'am, and running about. To start with, we watched them working on the dam and then Aleksei Nikolaich climbed a tree after a squirrel, right high-up, and began shaking the top of it. We all of us felt a bit frightened . . . The squirrel finally fell down and Treasure almost caught it . . . But it got away.

NATALYA PETROVNA [*glancing at Shpigelsky*]. And then what?

VERA. Then Aleksei Nikolaich made Kolya a bow—and so quickly—and then he crept up to our cow in the meadow and suddenly jumped on its back—and the cow took fright and ran about and started bucking—and he was laughing so much [*She laughs as well.*], and then Aleksei Nikolaich wanted to make us a kite, and after that we came here.

NATALYA PETROVNA [*patting her cheek*]. A child, you're a perfect child, aren't you? What do you think, Shpigelsky?

SHPIGELSKY [*slowly and while looking at Natalya Petrovna*]. I agree with you.

NATALYA PETROVNA. There you are, then.

SHPIGELSKY. Surely that doesn't make any difference—on the contrary . . .

NATALYA PETROVNA. Do you really think so? [*To Vera.*] Well, did you have a very good time?

VERA. Yes, ma'am. Aleksei Nikolaich is such good fun.

NATALYA PETROVNA. Is that so, [*After a short silence.*] Verochka, how old are you? [*Vera looks at her with some astonishment.*] A child . . . just a child . . .

[*Enter Rakitin from the hall.*]

SHPIGELSKY [*fussily*]. Ah, I forgot, there's a coachman here who's ill and I haven't seen him yet . . .

NATALYA PETROVNA. What's wrong with him?

SHPIGELSKY. A fever. Still there's no danger whatever.

NATALYA PETROVNA [*as he goes*]. Are you staying for dinner with us, doctor?

SHPIGELSKY. If you'll allow me. [*Exits into the hall.*]

NATALYA PETROVNA. *Mon enfant, vous feriez bien de mettre une autre robe pour le diner . . .** [*Vera rises.*] Come to me. . . [*Kisses her on the forehead.*] A child, just a child.

> [*Vera kisses her hand and goes towards the study.*]

RAKITIN [*in a soft voice to Vera, giving a wink*]. I've sent everything necessary to Aleksei Nikolaich.

VERA [*under her breath*]. Thank you very much indeed, Mikhailo Aleksandrych. [*Exits.*]

RAKITIN [*approaching Natalya Petrovna. She gives him her hand. He instantly presses it*]. At last we're alone. Natalya Petrovna, tell me, what's the matter with you?

NATALYA PETROVNA. Nothing, Michel, nothing. And if there had been something, it's all over now. Do sit down. [*Rakitin sit down next to her.*] Who doesn't have moments? There are always clouds in the sky. Why are you looking at me like that?

RAKITIN. I am looking at you like this—because I'm happy.

NATALYA PETROVNA [*smiling at him in response*]. Open the window, Michel. How lovely it is in the garden! [*Rakitin rises and opens the window.*] How do you do, wind. [*She laughs.*] It was just waiting for the chance to come bursting in . . . [*Looking round.*] It's taken over the whole room. Now it'll never be driven out . . .

RAKITIN. You are yourself gentle and calm now, like an evening after a thunderstorm.

NATALYA PETROVNA [*repeating the last words thoughtfully*]. After a thunderstorm . . . Surely there wasn't a thunderstorm, was there?

RAKITIN [*nodding*]. It was gathering.

NATALYA PETROVNA. Really? [*Looking at him, after a short*

silence.] Do you know something, Michel, I can't imagine anyone kinder than you. Really and truly. [*Rakitin tries to stop her*.] No, don't interrupt. Let me say it. You're patient, devoted and constant. You do not change. I owe you a great deal.

RAKITIN. Natalya Petrovna, why are you telling me this now?

NATALYA PETROVNA. I don't know. I feel happy, I feel on holiday. Don't stop me from having my say.

RAKITIN [*pressing her hand*]. You're as kind as an angel.

NATALYA PETROVNA [*laughing*]. You wouldn't have said that this morning . . . But listen, Michel, you know me and you must forgive me. Our relationship is so pure and honest—and yet it isn't entirely natural. You and I have a right to look not only Arkady but everyone straight in the eyes . . . Yes, but . . . [*She grows thoughtful*.] That's why sometimes I feel bad and awkward, and I get mad, and I feel ready, like a child, to empty out all my annoyance on someone else, particularly on you . . . Does it make you feel angry to be singled out?

RAKITIN [*vivaciously*]. On the contrary . . .

NATALYA PETROVNA. Yes, occasionally you enjoy tormenting someone you love . . . someone you love . . . After all, like Tatyana, I can also ask: 'Why pretend?'*

RAKITIN. Natalya Petrovna, you . . .

NATALYA PETROVNA [*interrupting him*]. Yes, I can say I love you. But do you know something, Rakitin? You know what sometimes seems strange to me is that I love you—and it's such a lucid, such a peaceful feeling—and yet the feeling doesn't excite me . . . it warms me, but still . . . [*Vivaciously*.] You've never made me cry—I would've thought I should have . . . [*Breaking off*.] What does that signify?

RAKITIN [*a little sadly*]. Such a question requires no answer.

NATALYA PETROVNA [*thoughtfully*]. After all, we've known each other a long time.

RAKITIN. Four years. Yes, we're old friends.

NATALYA PETROVNA. Friends . . . No, you're more to me than a friend.

RAKITIN. Natalya Petrovna, please don't touch on this . . . I am frightened for my own happiness, as if it might vanish away under your touch.

NATALYA PETROVNA. No . . . No . . . No . . . The whole thing is that you're too kind-hearted. You indulge me too much . . . You've spoiled me. You're too kind-hearted, do you hear?

RAKITIN [*with a smile*]. I do hear, ma'am.

NATALYA PETROVNA [*looking at him*]. I don't know how you . . . I don't want any other happiness. Many people could envy me. [*Stretches out both hands to him.*] Isn't that so?

RAKITIN. I am in your power . . . Do whatever you like with me.

[*Islaev's voice is heard in the hall calling out: 'So you sent for him, did you?'*]

NATALYA PETROVNA [*rising quickly*]. It's him! I can't see him just now. Goodbye!

[*Exits into the study.*]

RAKITIN [*looking after her*]. What is this? The beginning of the end or simply the end? [*After a short pause.*] Or is it the beginning?

[*Enter Islaev with a worried look and taking off his hat.*]

ISLAEV. Good day to you, Michel.

RAKITIN. We've already said hello to each other today.

ISLAEV. Ah, forgive me . . . I've been up to my eyes in work. [*Walks to and fro about the room.*] It's a strange business! The Russian peasant is very sensible, very quick in the uptake and I have great respect for him . . . But there are times when you can say something to him and say it again and explain and explain again—you think it's all clear and yet it's not the least bit of good. A Russian peasant hasn't got that . . . that . . .

RAKITIN. Are you still worried over the dam?

ISLAEV. That . . . so to say . . . that love for his work. It's precisely love that's missing. He will not let you express your opinion properly. 'Yes, master, yes, I'm listenin',' he says, but what sort of listening is it when he's not understood a thing? Look at the way the German works, that's another matter! A Russian hasn't enough patience. With all that, I still have great respect for him . . . But where's Natasha? Do you know?

RAKITIN. She was here a moment ago.

ISLAEV. What time is it? It should be time for dinner. I've been on my feet since this morning, there've been so many things to do. But I still haven't had time today to visit the building-site. Time literally slips by. The trouble is one simply doesn't seem to be able to get anywhere! [*Rakitin smiles.*] I see you're laughing at me—but, my dear fellow, what can I do? It's the way one is. I am a positive man, born to be in charge of things—and that's all. There was a time when I dreamed of something else. I came to nothing, my dear fellow! I got my fingers burnt—yes, indeed I did! Isn't Belyaev here?

RAKITIN. Who is Belyaev?

ISLAEV. Our new teacher, a Russian one. Shy as anything—still, he'll get used to things. The young fellow's no fool. I asked him today to see how the building was going on . . .

[*Enter Belyaev.*]

Ah, there he is! Well, how is it? What's going on there? Very likely they're not doing anything, eh?

BELYAEV. No, sir. They're working.

ISLAEV. Have they finished the second stage?

BELYAEV. They're on the third.

ISLAEV. About the beams—did you tell them?

BELYAEV. I told them.

ISLAEV. Well, what did they say?

BELYAEV. They said they'd never done it any different.

ISLAEV. Hmm. Was Yermil the carpenter there?

BELYAEV. He was there.

ISLAEV. Ah! Well, thank you very much. [*Enter Natalya Petrovna.*] Ah! Natasha! Good day!

RAKITIN. Why is it today you're saying hello to people twenty times over?

ISLAEV. As I told you, I've been up to my eyes in work. Ah, that reminds me! I haven't shown you my new winnower, have I? Let's go and see it. It's a marvel. Just imagine—the machine sets up a hurricane, quite simply a hurricane. There'll be time before dinner. Would you like to?

RAKITIN. Certainly.

ISLAEV. And you, Natasha, won't you come with us?

NATALYA PETROVNA. As if I knew anything about winnowing machines! You go off by yourselves—and see you're not late.

ISLAEV [*exiting with Rakitin*]. We won't be a moment . . .

[*Belyaev is on the point of leaving with them.*]

NATALYA PETROVNA [*to Belyaev*]. Where are you off to, Aleksei Nikolaich?

BELYAEV. I, ma'am . . . I . . .

NATALYA PETROVNA. However, if you'd like to go out . . .

BELYAEV. No, ma'am, I've spent the whole day outside.

NATALYA PETROVNA. Ah, well, in that case, sit down. Sit here. [*Indicating a chair.*] You and I haven't yet had a proper chat, Aleksei Nikolaich. We haven't yet got to know each other. [*Belyaev bows and sits down.*] And I'd like to get to know you.

BELYAEV. I, ma'am . . . I'm very flattered.

NATALYA PETROVNA [*with a smile*]. You're a bit frightened of me, I can see that. But in a little while, when you've got to know me, you'll stop being frightened of me. Tell me . . . tell me, how old are you?

BELYAEV. Twenty-one, ma'am.

NATALYA PETROVNA. Are your parents alive?

BELYAEV. My mother's dead. My father's still alive.

NATALYA PETROVNA. Has your mother been dead for long?

BELYAEV. A long time, ma'am.

NATALYA PETROVNA. But you can still remember her?

BELYAEV. Of course, ma'am, I remember her.

NATALYA PETROVNA. Does your father live in Moscow?

BELYAEV. No, ma'am—in the country.

NATALYA PETROVNA. Ah! Do you have any brothers or sisters?

BELYAEV. One sister.

NATALYA PETROVNA. Are you very fond of her?

BELYAEV. Yes, ma'am. She is much younger than me.

NATALYA PETROVNA. What is her name?

BELYAEV. Natalya.

NATALYA PETROVNA [*vivaciously*]. Natalya? Isn't that odd? I'm called Natalya too . . . [*Stops.*] And you're very fond of her, are you?

BELYAEV. Yes, ma'am.

NATALYA PETROVNA. Tell me, how do you find my Kolya?

BELYAEV. He is a very nice boy.

NATALYA PETROVNA. That's right. And so loving! He's already quite devoted to you.

BELYAEV. I'm ready to do what I can . . . I'm glad to . . .

NATALYA PETROVNA. You see, Aleksei Nikolaich, I would of course only want to make of him a person who was sensible and practical. I don't know whether I'll succeed, but in any case I would like him always to remember his boyhood with pleasure. The chief thing is—let him grow up free. I was brought up differently, Aleksei Nikolaich. My father was not a wicked man, but he was irritable and stern. Everyone at home, not least my dear mother, was frightened of him. My brother and I would cross each other secretly whenever we were summoned to see him. Sometimes my father took it upon himself to show me how fond he was, but I remember that even when he kissed me I froze stiff. My brother grew up—and you may have heard how he broke with his father . . . I'll never forget that terrible day! . . . Right up to his death I remained an obedient daughter. He used to call me his comfort, his Antigone—towards the end of his life he went blind—but all his tenderness could not wipe away the first impressions I had when I was a child. I was frightened of him, the blind old man, and in his presence I never felt free. Traces of that shyness, of that longstanding enforced restraint have perhaps not completely vanished even now. I know that at first glance I may seem—how can I put it?—cold perhaps . . . But I realize I'm telling you about myself instead of talking to you about Kolya. I only wanted to say that I know from personal experience how good it is for a child to grow up free. Take yourself, you had a free childhood, I imagine, didn't you?

BELYAEV. How can I put it, ma'am . . . Of course, I was quite free . . . No one bothered with me at all.

NATALYA PETROVNA [shyly]. Your father must surely have . . .

BELYAEV. It wasn't his sort of thing, ma'am. He spent all his time visiting the neighbours. On business, ma'am . . . Or not just on business, but . . . It was through them, one might say, he earned his daily bread. Through the things he could do for them.

NATALYA PETROVNA. I see! And as a result no one bothered with your education?

BELYAEV. Truth to tell, no one. Besides, it must be obvious. I am only too well aware of my inadequacies.

NATALYA PETROVNA. Perhaps . . . but on the other hand . . . [*She stops and continues in some confusion.*] Oh, by the way, Aleksei Nikolaich, was it you singing in the garden yesterday?

BELYAEV. When, ma'am?

NATALYA PETROVNA. Yesterday evening, beside the pond, was it you?

BELYAEV. Yes, ma'am. [*Hurriedly.*] I didn't think—the pond's such a long way from here—I didn't think anyone could hear from here . . .

NATALYA PETROVNA. You're not apologizing, are you? You have a very fine, strong voice and you sing so well. Have you studied music?

BELYAEV. Not at all, ma'am. I sing because I have an ear for music, ma'am—only simple songs.

NATALYA PETROVNA. You sing them beautifully . . . One of these days I'll ask you—not now, but when we get to know each other better, when we're friends—surely we can be friends, can't we, Aleksei Nikolaich? I feel I can trust you, the way I've been talking to you can show you that . . .

[*She stretches out her hand to him so that he can shake it. Belyaev takes it uncertainly and after some embarrassment, not knowing what to do with her hand, kisses it. Natalya Petrovna goes red and withdraws it. At that moment enter Shpigelsky from the hall. He stops and takes a step back. Natalya Petrovna stands up quickly and so does Belyaev.*]

NATALYA PETROVNA [*in confusion*]. Oh, it's you, doctor . . . Aleksei Nikolaich and I are here, you see . . . [*She stops.*]

SHPIGELSKY [*loudly and over-confidently*]. Just imagine, Natalya Petrovna, what's going on round here. I go to the servants' quarters and ask after the sick coachman and—lo and behold!—there's my patient sitting at a table with both cheeks stuffed full of onion pancake. With that going on, just you take up medicine and put your faith in illness and the chance of a decent living!

NATALYA PETROVNA [*with a forced smile*]. Really, well, well! . . . [*Belyaev is about to go.*] Aleksei Nikolaich, I forgot to mention to you . . .

VERA [*running in from the hall*]. Aleksei Nikolaich! Aleksei Nikolaich! [*She stops short suddenly at the sight of Natalya Petrovna.*]

NATALYA PETROVNA [*in some surprise*]. What is it? What do you want?

VERA [*reddening and lowering her eyes while pointing at Belyaev*]. Someone wants him.

NATALYA PETROVNA. Who?

VERA. Kolya—that is, Kolya was asking me about the kite . . .

NATALYA PETROVNA. Oh! [*In a low voice to Vera.*] On n'entre pas comme cela dans une chambre . . . Cela ne convient pas.* [*Turning to Shpigelsky.*] What time is it, doctor? Our clock is not always right. It's time we had dinner.

SHPIGELSKY. Let me see. [*Takes a watch out of his pocket.*] The time now, ma'am, is . . . The time is, I can inform you—twenty past four.

NATALYA PETROVNA. So you see! It *is* time! [*She goes over to the mirror and adjusts her hair. In the meantime Vera is whispering something to Belyaev. They both laugh. Natalya Petrovna sees them in the mirror. Shpigelsky glances at her sideways.*]

BELYAEV [*laughing, in a low voice*]. Not really?

VERA [*nodding, also in a low voice*]. Yes, yes, she just fell right down!

NATALYA PETROVNA [*turning to Vera with feigned indifference*]. What's that? Who fell down?

VERA [*in confusion*]. No ma'am . . . It's simply that Aleksei

Nikolaich put up a swing and nanny took it into her head to . . .

NATALYA PETROVNA [*without waiting for the end of the answer, speaking to Shpigelsky*]. Ah, by the way, Shpigelsky, I'd like to have a word with you . . . [*She leads him to one side and turns again to Vera.*] She didn't hurt herself, did she?

VERA. Oh, no, not at all!

NATALYA PETROVNA. I see . . . Still, Aleksei Nikolaich, you shouldn't have . . .

MATVEI [*enters from the hall and announces*]. Dinner is served, madam.

NATALYA PETROVNA. Ah! But where's Arkady Sergeich? He and Mikhailo Aleksandrovich will be late again.

MATVEI. They're already in the dining-room, madam.

NATALYA PETROVNA. And my mother?

MATVEI. She's also in the dining-room, madam.

NATALYA PETROVNA. Ah! Well, then, let's go. [*Pointing to Belyaev.*] Vera, allez en avant avec monsieur.*

[*Exit Matvei, followed by Belyaev and Vera.*]

SHPIGELSKY [*to Natalya Petrovna*]. You wanted to say something to me?

NATALYA PETROVNA. Oh, yes, I did . . . You see . . . we'll have to have a discussion about . . . about your proposal.

SHPIGELSKY. You mean—about Vera Aleksandrovna?

NATALYA PETROVNA. Yes. I'll think about it . . . I'll think about it.

[*They both go out into the hall.*]

ACT TWO

The scene is a garden. To left and right, beneath trees, are small benches. Directly in front are some raspberry canes. Enter KATYA *and* MATVEI *from the right.* KATYA *is carrying a basket.*

MATVEI. So what about it, Katerina Vasilevna? Be so good as to say what you mean at long last, I do earnestly beg you.

KATYA. Matvei Yegorych, I really . . .

MATVEI. Katerina Vasilevna, you know only too well how, so to speak, well-disposed I am to you. Of course, I am older than you in years. One definitely cannot argue about that. But I can still stand up for myself, I am still in my prime. I am also, I would have you know, a man of mild character. What more can you ask for?

KATYA. Matvei Yegorych, believe me, I feel very much for you and I am very grateful, Matvei Yegorych . . . But you see . . . You see I think we ought to wait a bit.

MATVEI. But what on earth should we wait for, Katerina Vasilevna? Previously, I would remind you, you wouldn't have said such a thing. As for the matter of respect, I think I can guarantee that. You will receive such respect, Katerina Vasilevna, that one couldn't ask for better. Besides, I am not a drinking man and, well, I've not heard a single complaint from any of my employers.

KATYA. Really, Matvei Yegorych, I don't know what I ought to say to you

MATVEI. Oh, Katerina Vasilevna, it's only quite recently that you've begun talking like this . . .

KATYA [*slightly reddening*]. How—recently? What d'you mean—recently?

MATVEI. I don't know . . . except that before . . . before
you treated me differently.

KATYA [*glancing into the wings, hurriedly*]. Take care—it's
that German coming.

MATVEI [*in annoyance*]. Damn him, that long-nosed, long-
legged old crane! . . . I'll talk to you later. [*Exit to the
right.*]

   [*Katya is also about to go into the raspberry canes. Enter
   Schaaf from the left, with a fishing rod over his shoulder.*]

SCHAAF [*following after Katya*]. Vere you go? Vere you go,
Katerine?

KATYA [*stopping*]. I have to pick some raspberries, Adam
Ivanych.

SCHAAF. R-arspberry? R-arspberry ist nice frucht. You
like r-arspberry?

KATYA. Yes, I do.

SCHAAF. Ha, ha! . . . and I . . . and I too. I like everysing
vot you like. [*Noticing that she wants to go.*] Oh, Katerine,
vait a moment.

KATYA. I mustn't, sir . . . The housekeeper'll be angry.

SCHAAF. O, zat ist nossing! You see, I am off . . . [*Indicating
the fishing rod.*] How to say—to fish, you onderstand, fish,
take fishes, zat ist. You like fishes?

KATYA. Yes, sir.

SCHAAF. Ha, Ha! And I too, I too. You know vot I vill tell
you, Katerine—in German ist a leetle song. [*Sings.*]
'*Cathrinchen, Cathrinchen, wie lieb' ich dich so sehr!* . . .' It
means: O leetle Katrine, O leetle Katrine, how much I
luv you. [*Tries to put an arm round her.*]

KATYA. That's enough, that's enough, you ought to be
ashamed . . . There are people coming. [*Escapes into the
raspberry canes.*]

SCHAAF [*adopting a stern look, in a low voice*]. Das ist dumm
. . .*

[*Enter from the right Natalya Petrovna on Rakitin's arm.*]

NATALYA PETROVNA [*to Schaaf*]. Ah, Adam Ivanych, you are going fishing, are you?

SCHAAF. Zat ist so.

NATALYA PETROVNA. Where's Kolya?

SCHAAF. Viz Lisavet Bogdanovna—having piano lesson.

NATALYA PETROVNA. Ah, I see [*Looking round.*] Are you here by yourself?

SCHAAF. By meinself, ma'am.

NATALYA PETROVNA. You haven't seen Aleksei Niko-laich, have you?

SCHAAF. Not at all.

NATALYA PETROVNA [*after a pause*]. We'll come with you, Adam Ivanych, and watch you fishing. Do you mind?

SCHAAF. I em vezzy pleest.

RAKITIN [*in a low voice to Natalya Petrovna*]. What's the point of this?

NATALYA PETROVNA [*to Rakitin*]. Come on, come on, *beau ténébreux* . . .*

[*Exit all three to the right.*]

KATYA [*cautiously poking her head out of the raspberry canes*]. They've gone . . . [*She comes out a short way, stops and grows thoughtful.*] Phew, that German! [*Sighs and again starts picking raspberries, singing softly to herself.*]

> 'Not tar that boils, nor fire that burns,
> But 'tis the heart that fiercely yearns . . .'

And Matvei Yegorych was right! [*Goes on singing.*]

> 'But 'tis the heart that fiercely yearns
> Not for dear father nor mother dear . . .'

What a big raspberry! [*Goes on singing.*]

> 'Not for dear father nor mother dear . . .'

How hot it is! One can hardly breathe! [*Goes on singing.*]

> 'Not for dear father nor mother dear . . .

But yearns the heart for . . .'

[*Suddenly she looks about her, falls quiet and half hides herself behind a clump of raspberry canes. Enter from the left Belyaev and Verochka. Belyaev is carrying a kite.*]

BELYAEV [*passing near the raspberry canes, to Katya*]. Why've you stopped singing, Katya? [*Sings:*]

'But yearns the heart for lovely maid . . .'

KATYA [*going red*]. That's not what we sing.

BELYAEV. What then? [*Katya laughs and does not answer.*] What are you doing, picking raspberries? Let's have a taste.

KATYA [*giving him the basket*]. Take them all . . .

BELYAEV. Why all of them? Vera Aleksandrovna, would you like some? [*Vera takes some from the basket and so does he.*] Well, that's enough. [*He tries to hand back the basket to Katya.*]

KATYA [*pushing away his hand*]. Take them all, take them . . .

BELYAEV. No, thank you, Katya. [*He hands her the basket.*] Thank you. [*To Vera.*] Vera Aleksandrovna, let's sit down on one of the seats. See, [*pointing to the kite*] I've got to fix its tail. You can help me. [*Both go and sit on a bench. Belyaev gives her the kite to hold.*] Just there. See you hold it straight. [*He begins to attach the tail.*] Is there something wrong?

VERA. I can't see you.

BELYAEV. Why do you want to see me?

VERA. I mean I can't see how you're attaching the tail.

BELYAEV. Ah! Well, we'll stop. [*He arranges the kite so she can see what he's doing.*] Katya, why've you stopped singing? Please go on.

[*After a while Katya begins to sing in a low voice.*]

VERA. Tell me, Aleksei Nikolaich, have you sometimes done kite-flying in Moscow?

BELYAEV. They don't bother with flying kites in Moscow!

Hold the string steady—that's right. Do you think we've got nothing better to do in Moscow?

VERA. Then what do you do in Moscow?

BELYAEV. What do we do? We study, listen to professors.

VERA. What do they teach you?

BELYAEV. Everything.

VERA. You are probably very good at learning. Better than all the others.

BELYAEV. No, I'm not very good. Certainly not better than all the others! I'm lazy.

VERA. Why are you lazy?

BELYAEV. God knows! I was just born that way most likely.

VERA [*after a pause*]. Do you have men friends in Moscow?

BELYAEV. Of course. Oh, this string's not strong enough.

VERA. And do you love them?

BELYAEV. What on earth! Do you love your men friends?

VERA. My men friends . . . I haven't got any.

BELYAEV. I meant, do you love your girl friends?

VERA [*slowly*]. Ye-e-es.

BELYAEV. You have got girl friends, haven't you?

VERA. Yes—except I don't know why but . . . but lately I haven't thought about them much. I haven't even answered Liza Moshina and in her letter she said she was so keen to hear from me.

BELYAEV. How can you say you haven't any men friends—what am I?

VERA [*with a smile*]. Well, you—you're different. [*After a pause.*] Aleksei Nikolaich!

BELYAEV. What?

VERA. Do you write poetry?

BELYAEV. No. Why do you ask?

VERA. Just, you know ... [*After a pause.*] At boarding school we had a girl who wrote poetry.

BELYAEV [*pulling tight a knot with his teeth*]. You don't say! Was it good?

VERA. I don't know. She used to read it to us and we would cry.

BELYAEV. Why did you cry?

VERA. Out of pity. We felt so sorry for her!

BELYAEV. So you went to school in Moscow, did you?

VERA. In Moscow, at Mrs Bolius's. Natalya Petrovna took me away last year.

BELYAEV. Are you fond of Natalya Petrovna?

VERA. I like her, she's such a kind person. I like her very much.

BELYAEV [*with a grin*]. And aren't you just a bit frightened of her?

VERA [*also with a grin*]. A bit.

BELYAEV [*after a pause*]. Who sent you to boarding school?

VERA. Natalya Petrovna's mother—before she died. I grew up in her house. I'm an orphan.

BELYAEV [*letting his hands drop*]. Are you an orphan? And you don't remember either your father or mother?

VERA. No.

BELYAEV. My mother's dead, too. You and I are both orphans. Well, it can't be helped! There's no point in being depressed about it.

VERA. They say orphans soon make friends with each other.

BELYAEV [*looking into her eyes*]. Really? Is that what you think?

VERA [*also looking into his eyes and smiling*]. I think we'll soon be friends.

BELYAEV [*laughs and again goes to work on the kite*]. What I'd like to know is—how long have I been in these parts?

VERA. Today is the twenty-eighth day.

BELYAEV. What a memory you've got! Well, there it is—the kite's finished. Just look at that tail! We must go and find Kolya.

KATYA [*approaching them with her basket*]. Would you like some more raspberries?

BELYAEV. No, thank you, Katya. [*Katya silently goes away.*]

VERA. Kolya's with Lizaveta Bogdanovna.

BELYAEV. Fancy keeping a boy indoors on a day like this!

VERA. Lizaveta Bogdanovna would only get in our way . . .

BELYAEV. I wasn't talking about her . . .

VERA [*hurriedly*]. Without her Kolya couldn't come out with us . . . Still, she said all sorts of flattering things about you yesterday.

BELYAEV. Really?

VERA. Do you like her?

BELYAEV. She's not bad! So let her take snuff if she wants to! . . . Why are you sighing?

VERA [*after a pause*]. I don't know. How clear the sky is!

BELYAEV. Are you sighing because of that? [*A silence.*] Perhaps you're bored?

VERA. Me bored? No! I sometimes don't know why I sigh. I'm certainly not bored. On the contrary . . . [*After a pause.*] I don't know—maybe I'm not quite well. Yesterday I was going upstairs to get a book—and suddenly on the stairs, just imagine, I suddenly sat down and burst into tears. God knows why . . . And afterwards the tears kept on coming . . . What's it mean? Anyhow I don't feel bad . . .

BELYAEV. It's a growing pain. You're still growing. It happens often. That's why your eyes looked a bit puffy yesterday evening.

VERA. Did you notice?

BELYAEV. Of course.

VERA. You notice everything.

BELYAEV. Well, no . . . not everything.

VERA [*thoughtfully*]. Aleksei Nikolaich . . .

BELYAEV. What?

VERA [*after a pause*]. There was something I wanted to ask you, wasn't there? I've forgotten what it was.

BELYAEV. Are you as scatterbrained as all that?

VERA. No, but—oh, yes, this is what I wanted to ask! I think you told me once you had a sister.

BELYAEV. I do.

VERA. Tell me—do I look like her?

BELYAEV. Oh, no. You're much better looking than she is.

VERA. That can't be true! A sister of yours—I'd love to be in her position.

BELYAEV. What? You'd like to be living now in our tiny little house?

VERA. I didn't mean that . . . Do you really have a tiny little house?

BELYAEV. A very small one. Not like the one here.

VERA. Why should one need a lot of rooms?

BELYAEV. Why? You'll learn in due course why one needs rooms.

VERA. In due course . . . When?

BELYAEV. When you become a housewife yourself . . .

VERA [*thoughtfully*]. Do you think so?

BELYAEV. Just you wait and see. [*After a pause.*] So, shall we go and find Kolya, Vera Aleksandrovna, eh?

VERA. Why don't you call me Verochka?

BELYAEV. And you can call me Aleksei, can't you?

VERA. Why not . . . [*Suddenly giving a shudder.*] Oh!

BELYAEV. What is it?

VERA [*in a low voice*]. Natalya Petrovna is coming.

BELYAEV [*also in a low voice*]. Where?

VERA [*indicating with her head*]. There—along the path, with Mikhailo Aleksandrych.

BELYAEV [*standing up*]. Let's go and find Kolya. He must have finished his lesson by now.

VERA. Let's go . . . Otherwise I'm frightened she'll start scolding me . . .

[*They both stand up and exit rapidly to the left. Katya once again hides in the raspberry canes. Enter Natalya Petrovna and Rakitin from the right.*]

NATALYA PETROVNA [*stopping*]. Isn't that Mr Belyaev going off with Verochka?

RAKITIN. Yes, it's them . . .

NATALYA PETROVNA. They seem to be running away from us.

RAKITIN. Perhaps.

NATALYA PETROVNA [*after a pause*]. Anyhow I don't think that Verochka should be . . . well, on her own like that in the garden with a young man . . . Of course, she's just a child; but still it's not right . . . I'll have a word with her.

RAKITIN. How old is she?

NATALYA PETROVNA. Seventeen! She's already seventeen! . . . Oh, it's hot today. I'm tired. Let's sit down. [*They sit down on the bench where Vera and Belyaev had been sitting.*] Has Shpigelsky gone?

RAKITIN. Yes.

NATALYA PETROVNA. You were wrong not to keep him here. I don't know why that man took it into his head to become a provincial doctor . . . He is very amusing. He makes me laugh.

RAKITIN. I'd imagined today you weren't in the mood for laughter.

NATALYA PETROVNA. Why did you think that?

RAKITIN. I just did!

NATALYA PETROVNA. You mean because today I don't find emotional matters to my liking? Well, I warn you that today absolutely nothing is going to bother me!— But that doesn't stop me laughing, quite the contrary. Still, I have to discuss something with Shpigelsky.

RAKITIN. May I ask what?

NATALYA PETROVNA. No, you may not. In any case, you know everything I think and everything I do . . . It's very boring.

RAKITIN. Forgive me . . . I wasn't proposing to . . .

NATALYA PETROVNA. I'd like to keep something from you.

RAKITIN. Good heavens, it might seem from what you're saying that I know everything . . .

NATALYA PETROVNA [*interrupting him*]. Don't you?

RAKITIN. You're making fun of me.

NATALYA PETROVNA. You seriously mean you don't know everything that's going on inside me? In that case I am not going to congratulate you. What—a man who's observing me morning, noon and night . . .

RAKITIN. What is this—a reproach?

NATALYA PETROVNA. A reproach? [*After a pause.*] No, I can see now that you're not very perceptive.

RAKITIN. Perhaps . . . But since I am observing you morning, noon and night, let me make one observation . . .

NATALYA PETROVNA. About me? Certainly.

RAKITIN. You won't be annoyed?

NATALYA PETROVNA. Of course not! I might want to, but I won't.

RAKITIN. For some while, Natalya Petrovna, you have been in a constantly irritable state and this irritability of

yours is not of your own doing, it comes from inside you,
just as if you were engaged in a struggle with yourself
and literally didn't know what to do about it. Before I
went to stay with the Krinitsyns I hadn't noticed it. It's
a recent thing. [*Natalya Petrovna uses her parasol to make
marks in front of her.*] You sometimes sigh so deeply . . .
like someone who is tired, very tired, and can't find any
way of relaxing.

NATALYA PETROVNA. What conclusion have you
reached, then, Mister Observer?

RAKITIN. Me? None. But I'm disturbed by it.

NATALYA PETROVNA. I am humbly grateful to you for
your concern.

RAKITIN. Besides . . .

NATALYA PETROVNA [*with some impatience*]. Please change
the subject.

   [*There is a pause.*]

RAKITIN. Are you not intending to drive out anywhere
today?

NATALYA PETROVNA. No.

RAKITIN. Why not? It's lovely weather.

NATALYA PETROVNA. Just laziness. [*A pause.*] Tell me—
you know Bolshintsov, don't you?

RAKITIN. Our neighbour, Afanasy Ivanych?

NATALYA PETROVNA. Yes.

RAKITIN. What a thing to ask! It was only the day before
yesterday that we were playing *préférence* with him here.

NATALYA PETROVNA. What sort of a man is he, that's
what I'd like to know.

RAKITIN. Bolshintsov?

NATALYA PETROVNA. Yes, yes, Bolshintsov.

RAKITIN. I confess I'd never expected anything like this!

NATALYA PETROVNA [*impatiently*]. What hadn't you
expected?

RAKITIN. That you'd ever start asking questions about Bolshintsov. He is a stupid, fat, pompous man—yet one really can't think of anything nasty to say about him.

NATALYA PETROVNA. He's not quite so stupid and pompous as you think.

RAKITIN. Perhaps. I confess I haven't studied the gentleman all that closely.

NATALYA PETROVNA [*ironically*]. You haven't done any research on him?

RAKITIN [*with a forced smile*]. What has made you think I . . .

NATALYA PETROVNA. It was just a thought!

[*Again there is a pause.*]

RAKITIN. Look how beautiful, Natalya Petrovna, that dark-green oak is against the dark-blue sky! It is completely drowned in the sun's rays and what intense colours it has! What indomitable life and strength it has, particularly when you compare it with that young birch tree! It is literally on the point of vanishing in the brilliant light. Its tiny little leaves shine with a kind of liquid brilliance as if they're about to melt, and meanwhile it just looks so pretty . . .

NATALYA PETROVNA. Do you know something, Rakitin? I've been aware of this a long time . . . You have a very delicate feeling for the so-called beauties of nature and you talk about them very elegantly and very cleverly . . . so elegantly and cleverly that I imagine nature must be unspeakably grateful to you for your exquisitely happy expressions of endearment. You run after her like a powdered, perfumed marquis in high-heeled red shoes running after a pretty peasant girl . . . The only thing is I sometimes think that she simply cannot understand and appreciate your sensitive observations, just as a peasant girl wouldn't be able to understand the courtly civilities of a marquis. Nature is much simpler, even cruder, than you suppose, simply because—thank

God!—it is healthy ... Birch trees don't melt and collapse in swoons like neurotic ladies.

RAKITIN. *Quelle tirade*! Nature is healthy ... that's to say, in other words, I am sick.

NATALYA PETROVNA. You're not the only one who is sick, we're neither of us all that healthy.

RAKITIN. Oh, I also know the trick of saying unpleasant things to someone in the most inoffensive way! Instead of telling someone straight out: You're a fool! all you have to do is say with a pleasant smile: We're both of us such fools, aren't we?

NATALYA PETROVNA. Now you're offended. That's enough—what nonsense! I simply meant that we're both—you don't like the word 'sick'—that we're both old, very old.

RAKITIN. Why are we old? I don't think of myself as old.

NATALYA PETROVNA. Well, then, listen—here we are sitting here now ... perhaps just fifteen minutes ago, on this very seat, two genuinely young people were sitting.

RAKITIN. Belyaev and Verochka, you mean? Of course they're younger than we are. There's a few years difference between us, that's all. But that doesn't make us senile.

NATALYA PETROVNA. The difference between us is not just one of years.

RAKITIN. Ah, I understand! You envy them their ... *naïveté*, their freshness, their innocence—in short, their silliness ...

NATALYA PETROVNA. You think so? Ah, you think they're silly, do you? I see that for you everyone's silly today. No, you haven't understood me. In any case— silliness! There's nothing wrong with it! What's the good of having a fine intellect when it doesn't make things entertaining? There's nothing more tedious than a serious intellect.

RAKITIN. Hm. Why don't you like saying things straight

out, without beating about the bush? I don't entertain
you—that's what you mean. Why do you take it out on
intellect in general when you really mean sinful old me?

NATALYA PETROVNA. You haven't really quite grasped
. . . [*Katya emerges from the raspberry canes.*] What is it—
have you been picking some raspberries, Katya?

KATYA. Yes, ma'am.

NATALYA PETROVNA. Let's have a look . . . [*Katya goes
up to her.*] What lovely raspberries! Such red ones . . . But
your cheeks are even redder. [*Katya smiles and looks down.*]
Well, off you go! [*Exit Katya.*]

RAKITIN. There's another young person to your taste.

NATALYA PETROVNA. Of course. [*She stands up.*]

RAKITIN. Where are you going?

NATALYA PETROVNA. In the first place, I want to see
what Verochka is doing. It's time she was home. And
secondly, I confess I don't like the turn our conversation
has taken. It would be better if we put a stop for a time
to our discussion of nature and youth.

RAKITIN. You would perhaps prefer to walk alone?

NATALYA PETROVNA. In all honesty, yes. We'll see each
other again soon. Still, we part as friends, don't we? [*She
offers him her hand.*]

RAKITIN [*rising*]. Of course. [*Presses her hand.*]

NATALYA PETROVNA. Goodbye. [*She opens her parasol and
exits left.*]

RAKITIN [*walking to and fro for a short while*]. What's wrong
with her? [*After a pause.*] That's it—she's being capri-
cious! Or is she? I'd never noticed this in her before. On
the contrary, I haven't known a woman more balanced
in her behaviour than she is. What *is* the reason? [*Walks
about again and suddenly stops.*] Oh, how comic people are
who have only one idea in their head, one purpose and
preoccupation in their lives—like me, for instance. She
was telling the truth—if you study the trivial morning

noon and night you become trivial yourself . . . It's all
quite true, but I cannot live without her, in her presence
I am more than just happy, it's a feeling that can't just
be called happiness—I belong to her wholly and parting
from her would be for me, without any exaggeration,
exactly the same as parting with life. So what's wrong
with her? What do all these inner alarums and excursions
mean, all this involuntary bitterness in her words? Do I
begin to bore her? Hmm. [*Sits down.*] I have never
deceived myself. I know very well the sort of love she has
for me. But I had hoped that in time this calm feeling
would . . . I had hoped! Have I a right—dare I hope? I
admit my position's pretty comic—almost despicable. [*A
pause.*] Well, why go on like this? She is an honourable
woman and I am no Lovelace.* [*With a bitter smile.*]
Unfortunately. [*Quickly gets up.*] Well, that's enough of
that! Banish all this rubbish from my head! [*Walking
about.*] What a beautiful day it is today! [*A pause.*] How
well she needled me . . . My 'exquisitely happy'
expressions . . . She's very clever, especially when she's
in a bad mood. And why all this sudden genuflecting to
simplicity and innocence?. . . It's that Russian tutor—
she's been talking to me a lot about him. I confess I
can't see anything special in him. He's just a student,
like all students. Surely she can't be . . . It can't be! She's
in a bad mood—she doesn't know herself what she wants
and she takes it out on me. Children have been known to
beat their nannies . . . What a flattering comparison! But
there's no need to upset her. When this fit of restless
yearning is passed, she'll be the first to laugh at this
lanky fledgling, at this fresh-faced youth . . . Not a bad
explanation, that, Mikhailo Aleksandrych, my friend,
but is it right? God knows! We'll see. It's not the first
time that you, my dear fellow, after a long struggle with
yourself, have suddenly given up all conjectures and
deliberations and quietly folded your arms and meekly
awaited the inevitable. And meanwhile you've got to
admit you've felt thoroughly awkward and hurt . . .
That's always been your way of doing things . . . [*Looks*

round.] Ah, if isn't the man himself, our young man as ever is! He's come just at the right moment . . . I've still not had a proper word with him. We'll see what sort of a chap he is.

[*Enter Belyaev from the left.*]

Ah, Aleksei Nikolaich! You've come out for a walk in the fresh air, have you?

BELYAEV. Yes, sir.

RAKITIN. That's to say, I must admit that today the air is not quite fresh. The heat's terrible, but here, under these lime trees, in the shade, it's fairly bearable. [*A pause.*] Have you seen Natalya Petrovna?

BELYAEV. I've just this moment met her. She and Vera Aleksandrovna have gone into the house.

RAKITIN. Wasn't it you and Vera Aleksandrovna I saw here about half an hour ago?

BELYAEV. Yes, sir. We were out for a stroll.

RAKITIN. Ah! [*Takes him by the arm.*] Well, how do you like living in the country?

BELYAEV. I love the country. There's only one thing wrong with it—the hunting round here is poor.

RAKITIN. Are you a hunter?

BELYAEV. Yes, sir. And you?

RAKITIN. Me? No. I have to confess to being a poor shot. And I'm too lazy.

BELYAEV. I'm lazy too—except for going for strolls.

RAKITIN. I see! Are you too lazy to read?

BELYAEV. No, I love reading. I can't stand working for long periods. I particularly can't stand having to occupy myself with one and the same subject.

RAKITIN [*smiling*]. With talking to ladies, for example?

BELYAEV. Now you're making fun of me! I'm quite frightened of ladies . . .

RAKITIN [*in some confusion*]. Whatever makes you think I was making fun of you?

BELYAEV. I just thought . . . It doesn't matter! [*A pause.*] Tell me, where can I get powder round here?

RAKITIN. In the town, I think. It's sold there under the label of poppy seed. Do you want good-quality stuff?

BELYAEV. No, just rifle powder. It's not for a gun, it's so I can make fireworks.

RAKITIN. I see. You know how to . . .

BELYAEV. Yes. I've already chosen the place for them—beyond the pond. I've heard that in a week's time it'll be Natalya Petrovna's birthday. That'd be a good time.

RAKITIN. Natalya Petrovna will find such attentions on your part very pleasant . . . She likes you, Aleksei Niko-laich, I have to tell you.

BELYAEV. I'm very flattered . . . Ah, by the way, Mikhailo Aleksandrych, I think you receive a journal. Could you give it to me to read?

RAKITIN. Certainly, with pleasure. It has some good poetry in it.

BELYAEV. I don't like poetry.

RAKITIN. Why not?

BELYAEV. I just don't. Comic poetry seems to me affected and in any case there's not much of it; and poetry of feeling . . . I don't know—I can't somehow believe in it.

RAKITIN. You prefer fiction?

BELYAEV. Yes, sir, I like good fiction. But critical arti-cles—they're what really appeal to me.

RAKITIN. Why's that?

BELYAEV. A warm-hearted man writes them . . .*

RAKITIN. And you yourself—you're not a writer?

BELYAEV. Oh, no! There's no point in writing if you haven't got the talent. It only makes people laugh. And what's so astonishing—perhaps you'd be good enough to explain it to me—is that a man can be clever, but as soon as he picks up a pen all his most cherished ideas go straight out of the window! No, there's no point in writing. Just let's try and understand what's already been written!

RAKITIN. Do you know something, Aleksei Nikolaich? Not many young men have as much common sense as you.

BELYAEV. I humbly thank you for the compliment. [*A pause.*] I have chosen the place on the other side of the pond for the fireworks because I know how to make Roman candles which can float on water . . .

RAKITIN. That must look very beautiful. Forgive me, Aleksei Nikolaich, but let me ask you—do you know French?

BELYAEV. No. I translated Paul de Kock's novel *The Montfermeil Dairymaid** for fifty roubles—perhaps you heard about it? But I don't know a word of French. Just imagine—*quatre-vingt-dix* I translated as 'four-twenty-ten'. . . I needed the money, you see. But I regret it. I'd like to know French. It's my damned laziness. I'd like to read George Sand in French. Still, there's the pronunciation . . . How can I cope with the pronunciation—*an, on, en, ion* . . . Impossible!

RAKITIN. Well, that affliction can be alleviated . . .

BELYAEV. What time is it, may I ask?

RAKITIN [*looking at his watch*]. Half-past one.

BELYAEV. What's Lizaveta Bogdanovna keeping Kolya so long at his piano lesson for? I'm sure he's now dying to run about.

RAKITIN [*gently*]. After all, one has to learn things, Aleksei Nikolaich.

BELYAEV [*with a sigh*]. You needn't say that, Mikhailo Aleksandrych—and I shouldn't have to listen to it . . . Of course, not everyone's such a layabout as I am.

RAKITIN. Oh, that's enough . . .

BELYAEV. I should know . . .

RAKITIN. And I should also know, on the contrary and for sure, that precisely what you regard as an inadequacy in yourself—your lack of restraint, your freedom—is just what appeals to people.

BELYAEV. To whom?

RAKITIN. To Natalya Petrovna, for instance.

BELYAEV. Natalya Petrovna? It's just with her that I don't feel myself—as you put it—free.

RAKITIN. Ah! Really?

BELYAEV. Yes . . . And, when all's said and done, Mikhailo Aleksandrych, isn't education what counts most in a person? It's easy for you to talk . . . I honestly don't understand you . . . [Stops suddenly.] What's that? It sounds like a corncrake in the garden, doesn't it? [He is about to leave.]

RAKITIN. Perhaps . . . But where are you off to?

BELYAEV. To get my gun . . .

[He is about to exit into the wings on the left when Natalya Petrovna enters and meets him.]

NATALYA PETROVNA [seeing him and suddenly smiling]. Where are you going, Aleksei Nikolaich?

BELYAEV. I, ma'am, I'm . . .

RAKITIN. He's going for his gun. He heard a corncrake in the garden . . .

NATALYA PETROVNA. No, don't shoot in the garden, please. Let the poor bird live. Besides, you could frighten Granny.

BELYAEV. Your servant, ma'am.

NATALYA PETROVNA [laughing]. Oh, Aleksei Nikolaich, you ought to be ashamed! 'Your servant, ma'am'—what a thing to say! How can you talk like that? Oh, but wait a moment—Mikhailo Aleksandrovych and I will undertake your education . . . Yes, yes, we've already talked about you more than once . . . There's a real conspiracy against you, I warn you! You will allow me to undertake your education, won't you?

BELYAEV. Please . . . I, er . . .

NATALYA PETROVNA. In the first place, don't be shy, it doesn't suit you. Yes, we'll undertake your education. [*Pointing to Rakitin.*] We are old and you are a young man—isn't that true? Just you see how well it'll all work out! You'll teach Kolya and I . . . we'll teach you.

BELYAEV. I am very grateful to you.

NATALYA PETROVNA. All right, then. What were you talking about just now with Mikhailo Aleksandrych?

RAKITIN [*smiling*]. He was telling me how he had translated a French book without knowing a word of French.

NATALYA PETROVNA. Oh! Well, then, we'll teach you French. By the way, what have you done with your kite?

BELYAEV. I've taken it back to the house. I thought you, er . . . you didn't like it.

NATALYA PETROVNA [*in some confusion*]. What on earth made you think that? Because I told Verochka . . . because I took Verochka indoors? No, that was . . . No, you're wrong. [*Spiritedly.*] In any case, do you know what? Now Kolya must have finished his lesson. Let's go and fetch him and Verochka and the kite—would you like that? And then we'll all go down to the meadow, shall we?

BELYAEV. With pleasure, Natalya Petrovna.

NATALYA PETROVNA. Splendid! Well, let's be off. Come on. [*Holds out her arm to him.*] Yes, take my arm—you're so gauche. Let's be off . . . quickly.

[*They both exit swiftly to the left.*]

RAKITIN [*watching them go*]. What vivacity! What joy! I've never seen an expression like that on her face before. And such a sudden change! [*A pause.*] Souvent femme varie . . .* But as for me—I am decidedly not to her taste today.

That is clear. [*A pause.*] It'll be interesting to see what'll happen next. [*Slowly.*] Surely . . . [*Waves his hand.*] Oh, it couldn't be! But that smile, that welcoming, soft, bright-eyed look . . . Oh, God grant I shouldn't feel pangs of jealousy, especially senseless jealousy! [*Suddenly glances round.*] Well, well, well—what on earth's this?

[*Enter from the left Shpigelsky and Bolshintsov. Rakitin goes to meet them.*]

Hello, gentlemen. I confess, Shpigelsky, I hadn't expected to see you today . . . [*Shakes hands with them.*]

SHPIGELSKY. Yes, I hadn't expected to either . . . I myself hadn't imagined I'd be . . . You see, I'd gone to visit him. [*Indicates Bolshintsov.*] But there he was sitting in his carriage on the way here. Well, I immediately turned my shafts round and came back here with him.

RAKITIN. Well, welcome back.

BOLSHINTSOV. I was just about to come . . .

SHPIGELSKY [*interrupting*]. The servants told us that every-one was in the garden. At least, there was no one in the drawing-room . . .

RAKITIN. You mean you didn't meet Natalya Petrovna?

SHPIGELSKY. When?

RAKITIN. Just a moment ago.

SHPIGELSKY. No. We didn't come straight here from the house. Afanasy Ivanych wanted to see whether there were any mushrooms in the birch wood.

BOLSHINTSOV [*in confusion*]. I . . .

SHPIGELSKY. Well, we know how fond you are of brown mushrooms. So Natalya Petrovna has gone off to the house? Well, then, we'd better go back too.

BOLSHINTSOV. Of course.

RAKITIN. She went back to the house in order to get everyone to go out for a walk. I think they're going kite-flying.

SHPIGELSKY. Ah, a splendid idea! In weather like this one should get out for walks.

RAKITIN. You can stay here. I'll go and tell her you've arrived.

SHPIGELSKY. Why on earth should you be troubled . . . Please, Mikhailo Aleksandrych, don't . . .

RAKITIN. No, I have to, in any case . . .

SHPIGELSKY. Well, then, we won't detain you. We don't want any formalities, you know . . .

RAKITIN. Goodbye, gentlemen. [*Exits to the left.*]

SHPIGELSKY. Goodbye. [*To Bolshintsov:*] Well, Afanasy Ivanych . . .

BOLSHINTSOV [*interrupting him*]. Why did you take it into your head, Ignaty Ilych, to talk about mushrooms . . . I'm astonished: what mushrooms?

SHPIGELSKY. Surely you didn't want me to mention that my very own Afanasy Ivanych took fright, didn't want to come straight here and begged to go by a roundabout route?

BOLSHINTSOV. That's true . . . still, to mention mushrooms . . . I don't know, maybe I'm wrong . . .

SHPIGELSKY. I'm sure you're wrong, my friend. Here's what you ought to be thinking about. You and I've come here. We've done what you wanted. Watch out—don't go and get egg all over your face!

BOLSHINTSOV. But you told me, Ignaty Ilych, you said . . . I would like to know definitely what answer . . .

SHPIGELSKY. Dear, good Afanasy Ivanych, there are ten miles or so between here and your estate, and every three-quarters of a mile or so you asked me the same question at least three times . . . Haven't you had enough? Well, listen, I'll indulge you once and for all. Natalya Petrovna said to me: 'I . . .'

BOLSHINTSOV [*nodding*]. Yes . . .

SHPIGELSKY [*with annoyance*]. Yes . . . Well, what's 'Yes

. . .' mean? I haven't told you anything yet. 'I', she said, 'know very little about Mr Bolshintsov, but he seems to me a good man. On the other hand, I do not intend to put any pressure on Verochka. So let him come and visit us and if he earns . . .'

BOLSHINTSOV. Earns! She said 'earns', did she?

SHPIGELSKY. 'If he earns her favour, Anna Seménovna and I will not put any obstacles . . .'

BOLSHINTSOV. 'Will not put any obstacles'? That's what she said, is it? We will not put any obstacles?

SHPIGELSKY. Well, yes, yes, yes. What an odd fellow you are! 'We will not put any obstacles in the way of their happiness.'

BOLSHINTSOV. Hmm.

SHPIGELSKY. 'Their happiness'—yes. But take note, Afanasy Ivanych, what you've got to do now. Now what you've got to do is convince Vera Aleksandrovna herself that, for her, marriage to you will indeed be happiness. You've got to earn her favour.

BOLSHINTSOV [blinking]. Yes, yes, earn . . . exactly, I agree with you.

SHPIGELSKY. You wanted me to bring you here today. Well, let's see how you'll go about it.

BOLSHINTSOV. Go about it? Yes, yes, one must go about it, one must earn her favour, exactly. Only the thing is, Ignaty Ilych . . . Let me confess to you as to my best friend my one weakness: you see, I wanted you, as you've kindly put it, to bring me here today . . .

SHPIGELSKY. You didn't want, you demanded, absolutely demanded.

BOLSHINTSOV. Well, yes, all right, I agree with you. But look, at home I . . . exactly, at home I was ready for anything, but now shyness has got the better of me.

SHPIGELSKY. Why are you shy?

BOLSHINTSOV [*glancing at him from beneath his brows*]. It's the risk.

SHPIGELSKY. Wh-a-at?

BOLSHINTSOV. The risk. There's a big risk. I must confess to you, Ignaty Ilych, as to . . .

SHPIGELSKY [*interrupting him*]. As to your best friend . . . I know, I know . . . Well?

BOLSHINTSOV. Exactly, I agree with you. I must confess to you, Ignaty Ilych, that I . . . that in general with ladies, with the female sex as a whole, I have had, so to speak, very little to do. I confess to you candidly, Ignaty Ilych, I simply can't think what there is to talk about to a person of the female sex—and what is more alone—particularly a young girl.

SHPIGELSKY. You astonish me. I just don't know what one can't talk about to a person of the female sex, particularly a young girl, particularly alone.

BOLSHINTSOV. Well, yes, you . . . Good heavens, who am I compared to you? So, you see, that's why in this case I'd like to draw on your experience, Ignaty Ilych. They say in such matters it's the very devil to get started, so couldn't you, er—as a conversational opening, you know—let me have some nice little thing to say, like a remark or something—and then I'd be my way. Then I'd be able to go on by myself.

SHPIGELSKY. I'm not going to let you have anything of the kind, Afanasy Ivanych, because no nice little thing to say will be any use to you. But I can give you some advice, if you like.

BOLSHINTSOV. Oh, please, my dear fellow, please be so good . . . As for my gratitude, you know what I . . .

SHPIGELSKY. That's enough, d'you think I'm doing a deal with you?

BOLSHINTSOV [*lowering his voice*]. About the little troika, you can rest assured.

SHPIGELSKY. That's enough! I say. Enough! Look, it's

like this, Afanasy Ivanych, you're undoubtedly a splendid chap in every way . . . [*Bolshintsov gives a slight bow*] a
man of excellent qualities . . .

BOLSHINTSOV. Oh, please, please . . .

SHPIGELSKY. Besides, I think you've got three hundred
serfs?

BOLSHINTSOV. Three hundred and twenty, my dear sir.

SHPIGELSKY. And they're not mortgaged?

BOLSHINTSOV. I don't owe a single penny.

SHPIGELSKY. Well, there you are! I told you you were a
most excellent chap and potential husband. But you've
been saying you've had very little to do with women . . .

BOLSHINTSOV [*sighing*]. Exactly, exactly. Since I was quite
small I can say, Ignaty Ilych, I've always fought shy of
the female sex.

SHPIGELSKY. Well, there you are! Mind you, it's no vice
in a man. But still, in some circumstances—for example,
when confessing your love to someone for the first time—
you've got to know how to say at least something or
other, haven't you?

BOLSHINTSOV. I entirely agree with you.

SHPIGELSKY. Otherwise Vera Aleksandrovna might just
think you're feeling unwell—and that would be that!
Besides, your figure, although in every respect present-
able, doesn't offer anything, you know, exceptional,
anything that strikes one particularly. Nowadays that's
what's needed.

BOLSHINTSOV [*sighing*]. Nowadays that's what's needed.

SHPIGELSKY. At least girls like that. Then, well, there's
your age . . . In short, you and I can't get by on charm
alone. So there's no point in having nice little things to
say. You can't rely on that. But you can rely on something else much more sure and effective—precisely your
personal qualities, my dear Afanasy Ivanych, and your
three hundred and twenty serfs. In your position I would
simply tell Vera Aleksandrovna . . .

BOLSHINTSOV. All on my own?

SHPIGELSKY. Certainly all on your own! 'Vera Aleksandrovna!' [*Judging by the movements of Bolshintsov's lips, he repeats every word after Shpigelsky.*] 'I love you and I ask for your hand in marriage. I am a kind, simple, quiet chap and I'm not poor. You will be entirely free when married to me. I will try to oblige you in every possible way. I ask you just to get to know something about me, to pay me a little more attention than you have done so far—and then give me your answer, as you like and when you like. I am prepared to wait, and I'll even consider it a pleasure.'

BOLSHINTSOV [*pronouncing the last word loudly*]. Pleasure. Yes, yes, yes, I agree with you. Except there's one thing, Ignaty Ilych—I think you were good enough to use the word 'quiet'. . . so to speak, a 'quiet chap'. . .

SHPIGELSKY. So what? Aren't you a quiet chap?

BOLSHINTSOV. Ye-es . . . But I still think, is that right and proper, Ignaty Ilych? Wouldn't it be better to say, for example . . .

SHPIGELSKY. What?

BOLSHINTSOV. For example . . . for example . . . [*A pause.*] Oh, very well, let's say 'quiet'!

SHPIGELSKY. Afanasy Ivanych, just listen to me a moment—the more simply you express yourself, the fewer colourful phrases you put into your speech, the better it'll be, believe me. But the chief thing is—don't insist on anything, don't lay down the law, Afanasy Ivanych. Vera Aleksandrovna is still very young and you could frighten her. Give her time to think over your proposal properly. Oh, yes, and another thing! I almost forgot to mention it. You've been good enough to allow me to give you some advice . . . well, it now and then happens, my dear Afanasy Ivanych, that you say things like 'troot' when you mean 'fruit' and 'hrost' when you mean 'frost'—all right, say 'troot' and 'hrost' if you like, but 'fruit' and 'frost' are more common, if you see what

I mean, they've come into regular use, as one might say. I remember you once said in my presence that a particular *bon viveur* of a landowner was a real *bonzhiban*. 'What a *bonzhiban* he is!' you said. A very good expression, of course, but unfortunately it doesn't mean anything. You know I'm not too well up in the French dialect, but I do know that much. Avoid fancy phrases and I'll guarantee you success. [*Looks round.*] Oh, look, there they are and they're all coming this way! [*Bolshintsov makes an attempt to leave.*] Where are you off to? Going mushrooming again? [*Bolshintsov smiles, goes red and stays where he is.*] The main thing is—don't be shy!

BOLSHINTSOV [*hurriedly*]. Surely Vera Aleksandrovna doesn't know anything about it yet?

SHPIGELSKY. Of course not!

BOLSHINTSOV. Anyhow, I trust you . . .

[*He blows his nose. Enter from the left: Natalya Petrovna, Vera, Belyaev with a kite, Kolya; behind them come Rakitin and Lizaveta Bogdanovna. Natalya Petrovna is in a good mood.*]

NATALYA PETROVNA [*to Bolshintsov and Shpigelsky*]. Ah, hello, gentlemen. Hello, Shpigelsky. I hadn't expected to see you today, but I'm always glad to see you. How do you do, Afanasy Ivanych?

[*Bolshintsov bows with a certain amount of embarrassment.*]

SHPIGELSKY [*to Natalya Petrovna, indicating Bolshintsov*]. You see this gentleman, he insisted on bringing me here . . .

NATALYA PETROVNA [*laughing*]. I'm very obliged to him. But surely you don't have to be forced to visit us, do you?

SHPIGELSKY. Heaven forbid! But . . . it was simply that this morning . . . coming from here—oh, heavens! . . .

NATALYA PETROVNA. Ah, he's tongue-tied! Our Mr Diplomat is tongue-tied!

SHPIGELSKY. It gives me very great pleasure, Natalya Petrovna, to see you in such a—so far as I can remark—such a buoyant frame of mind.

NATALYA PETROVNA. Ah, you feel you must remark on it! Is it so rare an occurrence in my case?

SHPIGELSKY. Oh, heavens, no . . .

NATALYA PETROVNA. *Monsieur le diplomate*, you are getting more and more mixed up.

KOLYA [*who has been all the while impatiently twisting and turning round Belyaev and Vera*]. *Maman, Maman*, when can we start flying the kite?

NATALYA PETROVNA. Whenever you like. Aleksei Nikolaich and you, Verochka, we'll go down to the meadow . . . [*Turning to the rest.*] I imagine you, lady and gentlemen, will not be too interested in kite-flying. Lizaveta Bogdanovna and you, Rakitin, I rely upon to look after our dear friend, Afanasy Ivanych.

RAKITIN. Why do you imagine, Natalya Petrovna, that we won't be interested in kite-flying?

NATALYA PETROVNA. You're a clever lot. Kite-flying ought to seem frivolous to you. However, it's as you like. We won't stop you coming with us . . . [*To Belyaev and Verochka.*] Let's go.

[*Natalya, Vera, Belyaev and Kolya exit to the right.*]

SHPIGELSKY [*to Bolshintsov, after glancing with some astonishment at Rakitin*]. Afanasy Ivanych, give Lizaveta Bogdanovna your arm, there's a good fellow.

BOLSHINTSOV [*hurriedly*]. I do so with great pleasure . . . [*Takes Lizaveta Bogdanovna by the arm.*]

SHPIGELSKY [*to Rakitin*]. Let's you and I walk together, Mikhailo Aleksandrych, if you'll permit. [*Takes him by the arm.*] Just see the way they're rushing off down the path! Let's go and see what the kite-flying's like, even though we are a clever lot . . . Afanasy Ivanych, will you be good enough to lead the way?

BOLSHINTSOV [*addressing Lizaveta Bogdanovna as they go*]. Today the weather is very, one might say, pleasant, isn't it?

LIZAVETA BOGDANOVNA [*affectedly*]. Oh, very!

SHPIGELSKY [*to Rakitin*]. And you and I, Mikhailo Aleksandrych, must have a talk . . . [*Rakitin suddenly laughs*] Why're you laughing?

RAKITIN. No . . . nothing really. I'm amused that we've become the rearguard.

SHPIGELSKY. An advance-guard, you know, can very quickly become a rearguard. It's all a matter of change of direction.

[*They all exit to the left.*]

ACT THREE

The scene is the same as for Act One. Enter RAKITIN *and* SHPIGELSKY *through the hall doors.*

SHPIGELSKY. So be a good fellow and help me, Mikhailo Aleksandrych.

RAKITIN. How can I help you, Ignaty Ilych?

SHPIGELSKY. How? For heaven's sake, Mikhailo Aleksandrych, look at it from my position. Of course, I'm actually on the side-lines in this business, I acted, one might say, more from a desire to oblige . . . Oh, my kind heart'll be the death of me!

RAKITIN [*laughing*]. Hardly the death of you, surely!

SHPIGELSKY [*also laughing*]. Too early to say, but still my position's really very awkward. I brought Bolshintsov here on the wishes of Natalya Petrovna and informed him of the answer with her permission, but now from one side I hear nothing but grumbling, just as if I'd done something silly, and on the other side Bolshintsov doesn't give me a moment's peace. They won't have anything to do with him and they won't speak to me . . .

RAKITIN. I can't think, Ignaty Ilych, what could have made you start on this business! After all, between ourselves, Bolshintsov is simply a fool.

SHPIGELSKY. You say: between ourselves! You're not giving anything away in saying that! And since when is it only people in their right minds who get married? You can put a ban on fools doing some things, but you can't ban them from marrying. You say I'd started on this business—not at all! It was like this: a friend asked me to put in a good word for him . . . Well, should I have refused? Eh? I'm a kind-hearted chap, I just don't know how to refuse. I do a friend a favour and then I'm told:

'I am most awfully, awfully grateful to you, but I don't want to hear any more about it'. . . I understand and I don't say anything more about it. Suddenly it's suggested to me that I should try again . . . I do and I'm in hot water. But what on earth have I done wrong?

RAKITIN. Who said you'd done wrong? I'm only surprised that you've gone to such trouble.

SHPIGELSKY. Gone to such trouble . . . The man won't let me have a moment's peace!

RAKITIN. Oh, well, that's enough of that!

SHPIGELSKY. Besides, he's my oldest friend.

RAKITIN [with an uncertain smile]. Really! Well, that's another matter.

SHPIGELSKY [also smiling]. However, I won't pretend to you—you're not easily deceived. Well, yes—he promised me . . . my trace horse got a nail in its foot . . . he promised me . . .

RAKITIN. Another trace horse?

SHPIGELSKY. No, I confess, a whole troika.

RAKITIN. Ah, you should've said so at the start!

SHPIGELSKY [animatedly]. But please don't run away with the idea that . . . I, er, I would never have agreed to be a go-between in this matter—it's entirely against my nature—[Rakitin smiles.] if I hadn't known that Bolshintsov was the most honest of men. Still, all I want now is a definite answer—yes or no.

RAKITIN. Have things gone as far as that?

SHPIGELSKY. What on earth are you imagining? I'm not talking about marriage, only about coming here, about visiting rights . . .

RAKITIN. But who would object?

SHPIGELSKY. Object, you say! Of course, for anyone else . . . But Bolshintsov is as shy as they come, an innocent abroad, straight out of some Golden Age or other, mother's milk hardly yet dry . . . He has very little confidence in himself, needs a bit of encouragement. Besides, his intentions are of the very best.

RAKITIN. And he has good horses.

SHPIGELSKY. And he has good horses. [*Takes some snuff and offers Rakitin his snuff-box*]. Would you care for some?

RAKITIN. No, thank you.

SHPIGELSKY. So that's it, Mikhailo Aleksandrych. I have no desire to mislead you, you see. And why should I? It's as plain as the palm of one's hand—an upright man, with money, a quiet chap: if he'll do—good; if he won't— then say so . . .

RAKITIN. It sounds excellent, I grant you. But where do I come in? I really can't see what I can do.

SHPIGELSKY. Oh, Mikhailo Aleksandrych! Surely we all know, don't we, that Natalya Petrovna has the greatest respect for you and even sometimes listens to what you have to say . . . Be a friend, Mikhailo Aleksandrych [*putting his arm round him*], put in a good word . . .

RAKITIN. And you really think he'd make a good husband for Verochka?

SHPIGELSKY [*assuming a serious expression*]. I'm convinced of it. You don't believe it—well, just you wait and see. After all, in marriage, as you know yourself, the chief thing is solidity of character. And you couldn't find anyone solider than Bolshintsov! [*Glances round.*] Ah, I think I see Natalya herself coming this way . . . My dear fellow, benefactor, father o'mine! For the sake of two chestnuts as trace horses and a bay between the shafts, do what you can!

RAKITIN [*smiling*]. Well, all right, all right . . .

SHPIGELSKY. See what you can do, I'm relying on you . . . [*Escapes into the hall.*]

RAKITIN [*watching him go*]. What a wheeler and dealer that doctor is! Verochka—and Bolshintsov! Well, so what? One can think of worse matches. I'll do what he asks, but as for *that*, it's not my affair!

[*He turns round. Enter Natalya Petrovna from the study, who stops on seeing him.*]

NATALYA PETROVNA [*indecisively*]. It's you . . . I thought you were in the garden . . .

RAKITIN. You don't appear to like seeing me here . . .

NATALYA PETROVNA [*interrupting him*]. Oh, that's enough! [*Advances downstage.*] Are you here all alone?

RAKITIN. Shpigelsky's only just left.

NATALYA PETROVNA [*slightly frowning*]. Ah, that provincial Talleyrand*. . . What's he been telling you? Is he still about?

RAKITIN. That provincial Talleyrand, as you call him, is evidently not in favour with you today . . . but yesterday I think he was . . .

NATALYA PETROVNA. He's fun and he's entertaining, true, but he will get mixed up in other people's affairs—and that's unpleasant. What's more, despite the way he's so deferential, he's very sharp-tongued and importunate. He's a tremendous cynic.

RAKITIN [*approaching her*]. You didn't say that about him yesterday.

NATALYA PETROVNA. Possibly. [*Animatedly*] So what was he talking to you about?

RAKITIN. He was talking to me about Bolshintsov.

NATALYA PETROVNA. Oh, about that fool!

RAKITIN. You didn't call him that yesterday.

NATALYA PETROVNA [*with a forced smile*]. Yesterday is not today.

RAKITIN. For everyone else, yes, but evidently not for me.

NATALYA PETROVNA [*lowering her eyes*]. What do you mean?

RAKITIN. For me today is the same as yesterday.

NATALYA PETROVNA [*holding out a hand to him*]. I understand your reproach, but you're wrong. Yesterday I

wouldn't have admitted that I owe you an apology ...
[*Rakitin appears about to stop her*] Don't please stop me ...
I know, and you know, what I mean—and today I admit
it. I've been giving it a lot of thought today. Believe me,
Michel, no matter what silly thoughts I may have had,
no matter what I might have said or done, there's no one
I rely on more than you. [*Lowering her voice.*] I don't love
anyone as much as I love you ...[*A moment's silence.*] You
don't believe me?

RAKITIN. I do believe you. But today you look sad. Is
there something wrong?

NATALYA PETROVNA [*not listening to him and continuing with
what she had been saying*]. It's only that I'm convinced of
one thing, Rakitin—one should never in any circumstances answer for oneself or put one's trust in anything.
We so often never understand what's happened in our
past ... so how can we possibly answer for what's going
to happen in the future? You can't take the future
captive.

RAKITIN. That's true.

NATALYA PETROVNA [*after a long silence*]. Please listen, I
want to be candid with you and perhaps I'll annoy you
slightly, but I know secrecy on my part would annoy you
even more. I confess to you, Michel, that that young
student—that Belyaev—has produced a fairly strong
impression on me ...

RAKITIN [*in a low voice*]. I knew that.

NATALYA PETROVNA. Ah, so you'd noticed! How long?

RAKITIN. Since yesterday.

NATALYA PETROVNA. Ah!

RAKITIN. The day before yesterday—remember?—I mentioned the change which had occurred in you. At the
time I didn't know what to ascribe it to. But yesterday
after our conversation—and down at the meadow—if
only you'd been able to see yourself! I didn't recognize
you—you'd literally become someone else! You were

laughing and jumping about and romping like a little girl, your eyes were shining, your cheeks were bright red and the delighted attention with which you looked at him, the way you smiled ... [*Glancing at her.*] You see, even now your face has brightened up as you think about it ... [*Turns away.*]

NATALYA PETROVNA. No, Rakitin, for God's sake don't turn away from me! Please listen. Why exaggerate? The young man infected me with his youthfulness, that's all. I was never young myself. Michel, from my girlhood right up to now—you know the whole story of my life, after all ... Out of inexperience it went to my head like wine, but I know it'll pass just as quickly as it came. It's hardly worth talking about! [*A moment's silence.*] Just please don't turn away from me, please don't take away your hand ... Please help me ...

RAKITIN [*in a low voice*]. Help ... What a cruel word that is! [*Loudly.*] Natalya Petrovna, you yourself don't know what's happening to you. You're sure it's not worth talking about and yet you ask for help—evidently you feel you need it!

NATALYA PETROVNA. That's to say ... Yes ... I'm turning to you as a friend.

RAKITIN [*bitterly*]. Ye-e-s ... Natalya Petrovna, I am ready to justify your faith in me, only ... only give me a moment to pluck up courage ...

NATALYA PETROVNA. Pluck up courage! Surely there's nothing unpleasant threatening, is there? Surely nothing's changed?

RAKITIN [*bitterly*]. Oh, no, everything's as it was!

NATALYA PETROVNA. What are you thinking, Michel? You can hardly suppose ...

RAKITIN. I don't suppose anything.

NATALYA PETROVNA. You can hardly despise me as much as all that ...

RAKITIN. Stop, for God's sake! It'd be better if we talked

about Bolshintsov. The doctor is awaiting an answer about Verochka, you know.

NATALYA PETROVNA [*sadly*]. You're angry with me.

RAKITIN. Oh, no, I'm not! But I'm sorry for you.

NATALYA PETROVNA. That really is hurtful. Michel, you ought to be ashamed . . . [*Rakitin is silent. She shrugs and continues in a tone of annoyance.*] You say the doctor is awaiting an answer? Who asked him to get mixed up . . .

RAKITIN. He told me you did . . .

NATALYA PETROVNA [*interrupting him*]. Perhaps, perhaps, although I don't think I told him anything definite . . . In any case, I can change my mind. And anyhow, my God, what's it matter? Shpigelsky involves himself in all sorts of things, in his wheeling and dealing he won't succeed every time.

RAKITIN. He simply wants to know what the answer is . . .

NATALYA PETROVNA. What the answer is . . . [*After a pause.*] Michel, that's enough, give me your hand . . . Why such a look of indifference, why such cold politeness? What have I done wrong? Just consider a moment, is it really my fault? I came to you hoping to receive some kindly advice, I didn't hesitate an instant, I didn't dream of hiding anything from you, but you . . . I see I shouldn't have been so frank with you. It wouldn't have entered your head. You didn't suspect anything . . . and you've deceived me. And God knows what you must be thinking now!

RAKITIN. What I'm . . . ? Really!

NATALYA PETROVNA. Please give me your hand . . . [*He does not move. She continues in a rather hurt voice.*] Are you definitely turning away from me? Watch out, then, it'll be the worse for you. Still, I'm not blaming you . . . [*Bitterly.*] You're just jealous!

RAKITIN. I have no right to be jealous, Natalya Petrovna. You can't be serious.

NATALYA PETROVNA [*after a pause*]. As you wish. So far

as Bolshintsov is concerned, I haven't yet spoken to Verochka.

RAKITIN. I can send her to you now.

NATALYA PETROVNA. Why now? Still, if you want to . . .

RAKITIN [*moving towards the door of the study*]. Shall I send for her?

NATALYA PETROVNA. Michel, for the last time . . . You said a moment ago you felt sorry for me. All right, then, feel sorry! Surely, though . . .

RAKITIN [*coldly*]. Shall I?

NATALYA PETROVNA [*with annoyance*]. Yes.

[*Exit Rakitin into the study. Natalya Petrovna remains motionless a short while, sits down, picks up a book from the table, opens it and lets it fall into her lap.*] Him, too! What is going on? Him . . . him, too! I was relying on him. What about Arkady? My God, I'd forgotten about him! [*She sits up straight.*] I see the time's come to put an end to it all.

[*Enter Vera from the study.*]

Yes, the time's come . . .

VERA [*shyly*]. You were asking for me, Natalya Petrovna?

NATALYA PETROVNA [*quickly looking round*]. Ah, Verochka! Yes, I was asking for you.

VERA [*going up to her*]. Are you all right?

NATALYA PETROVNA. Me? Yes. Why do ask?

VERA. It seemed to me you might . . .

NATALYA PETROVNA. No, I'm all right. A bit hot, that's all. Do sit down. [*Vera sits down.*] Listen, Vera, you're not busy now, are you?

VERA. No, ma'am.

NATALYA PETROVNA. I'm asking you because I want to have a talk with you—a serious talk. You see, my dear, until now you've still been a child. But you're seventeen and you're intelligent—it's time you were thinking about your future. You know I love you like a daughter. My

home will always be your home. But still, in other
people's eyes, you're an orphan and you're not rich. With
time you may get bored living forever with strangers.
Listen—would you like to be mistress, absolute mistress
in your own home?

VERA [*slowly*]. I do not understand you, Natalya Petrovna.

NATALYA PETROVNA [*after a pause*]. Someone is asking
me for your hand. [*Vera looks at Natalya Petrovna with
astonishment.*] You hadn't been expecting this. I confess
that to me personally it seems rather strange. You're still
so young . . . I don't have to tell you that I don't intend
to put any pressure on you at all. In my opinion, it's too
soon for you to get married. I simply thought it my duty
to inform you . . . [*Vera suddenly covers her face with her
hands.*] Vera, what is it? Are you crying? [*Takes her by the
arm.*] Why are you trembling? You're not frightened of
me, Vera, are you?

VERA [*in a hollow voice*]. I'm at your mercy, Natalya
Petrovna.

NATALYA PETROVNA [*taking Vera's hands away from her
face*]. Vera, aren't you ashamed to be crying? Aren't you
ashamed to say you're at my mercy? What do you take
me for? I am talking to you as a daughter, but you . . .
[*Vera kisses her hands.*] Ah, you're at my mercy, are you?
In that case, please give me a smile this minute . . . I
order you to . . . [*Vera smiles through her tears.*] That's
better. [*Natalya Petrovna puts an arm round her and draws her
to her.*] Vera, my poor child, behave with me just as you
would with your own mother—or, better still, imagine
I'm your older sister and let's have a chat together about
all these marvellous things . . . Would you like that?

VERA. I'm ready, ma'am.

NATALYA PETROVNA. Well, then, listen a moment . . .
Come a bit closer. That's right. In the first place, because
you're my sister, let's suppose I don't have to assure you
that you are quite at home here—with eyes like yours
you'd be at home anywhere. So it shouldn't so much as

enter your head that you're a burden to anyone in the world and that anyone wants to get rid of you . . . Are you listening? But one fine day your sister comes to you and says: Imagine what, Vera, someone has asked for your hand in marriage—well, what would you answer her? That you're still very young and you haven't even thought about getting married?

VERA. Yes, ma'am.

NATALYA PETROVNA. You mustn't say 'ma'am' to me. Sisters don't say 'ma'am' to each other, do they?

VERA [smiling]. Well . . . yes.

NATALYA PETROVNA. Your sister'll agree with you, the suitor'll be refused and that'll be the end of it. But if the suitor is a good man, someone with money, if he's prepared to wait, if he's only asking to be allowed to see you from time to time, in the hope that with time you'll grow to like him . . .

VERA. Who is he?

NATALYA PETROVNA. Ah, you're curious! You haven't guessed?

VERA. No.

NATALYA PETROVNA. You've seen him today . . . [Vera goes red.] True, he's not very good-looking and he's not very young . . . Bolshintsov.

VERA. Afanasy Ivanych?

NATALYA PETROVNA. Yes . . . Afanasy Ivanych.

VERA [gazes a short while at Natalya Petrovna, suddenly starts laughing and then stops]. You're serious?

NATALYA PETROVNA [smiling]. Yes . . . But I can see there's nothing doing for Bolshintsov round here. If you'd burst into tears at his name, then he could still have hoped, but you burst out laughing. There's only one thing for him now—to wish him Godspeed back to where he came from.

VERA. Forgive me, but I really hadn't expected . . . Do people really get married at his age?

NATALYA PETROVNA. What on earth are you thinking about? How old is he? He's not yet fifty. He's in his prime.

VERA. Perhaps . . . But he's got such a funny face . . .

NATALYA PETROVNA. Well, that's enough about him. He's over and done with, God be with him! Still, it's understandable that a girl your age wouldn't want a man like Bolshintsov. You want to marry for love, not out of cold calculation, don't you?

VERA. Yes, Natalya Petrovna . . . and didn't you get married to Arkady Sergeich for love, too?

NATALYA PETROVNA [after a pause]. Of course, for love. [After another pause and after squeezing Vera's hand.] Yes, Vera . . . I've just called you a girl, but girls know what's right. [Vera lowers her eyes.] So it's decided. Boshintsov is put out to grass. I confess I wouldn't myself have found it very nice to see his puffy old face next to your fresh pretty one, although he's a very good man, you know. So you see now you were wrong to be frightened of me. How quickly everything's been settled! [Reproachfully.] Really you behaved as if I were your benefactress! You know how I hate that word . . .

VERA [embracing her]. Forgive me, Natalya Petrovna.

NATALYA PETROVNA. All right, all right . . . Are you really frightened of me?

VERA. No. I love you. I'm not frightened of you.

NATALYA PETROVNA. Well, I'm thankful for that. So let's suppose we're now great friends and don't hide anything from each other. If I were to ask you, Verochka, to tell me by whispering in my ear . . . you don't want to marry Bolshintsov simply because he's much older than you and not good-looking, is that it?

VERA. Isn't that enough, Natalya Petrovna?

NATALYA PETROVNA. Oh, I agree . . . But there's no other reason?

VERA. I don't know him at all . . .

NATALYA PETROVNA. Quite true, but you're not answering my question.

VERA. There's no other reason.

NATALYA PETROVNA. Really? In that case I'd advise you to think again. It's hard to love Bolshintsov, I know, but, I repeat, he's a good man. You see, if you'd been in love with someone else—well, then it would have been a different matter. But so far you haven't had any word from your heart, have you?

VERA [shyly]. What d'you mean, ma'am?

NATALYA PETROVNA. You're not in love with anyone yet?

VERA. I love you . . . and Kolya. I also love Anna Semënovna.

NATALYA PETROVNA. No, I'm not talking about that kind of love, you haven't understood me. For example, of all the young men you could have seen here or at parties elsewhere, isn't there one you've been fond of?

VERA. No, ma'am . . . I've liked some, but . . .

NATALYA PETROVNA. For example, I noticed that at the evening at the Krinitsyns you danced three times with that tall officer—what was his name?

VERA. With an officer?

NATALYA PETROVNA. Yes, he had such large whiskers.

VERA. Oh him! No, I didn't like him.

NATALYA PETROVNA. Well, what about Shalansky?

VERA. Shalansky is a nice man, but he . . . I don't think he's interested in me.

NATALYA PETROVNA. Why not?

VERA. I think he . . . he thinks more about Liza Belskaya.

NATALYA PETROVNA [*glancing at her*]. Ah, so you've noticed that! [*Silence.*] Well, what about Rakitin?

VERA. I am very fond of Mikhailo Aleksandrovich . . .

NATALYA PETROVNA. Yes, like a brother . . . And what about Belyaev?

VERA [*reddening*]. Aleksei Nikolaich? I like Aleksei Nikolaich.

NATALYA PETROVNA [*observing Vera closely*]. Yes, he's a good man. Except he's so distant with everyone . . .

VERA [*innocently*]. No, ma'am, he's not distant with me.

NATALYA PETROVNA. Ah!

VERA. He talks to me, ma'am. Perhaps it just seems to you he's like that . . . He's afraid of you. He hasn't yet got to know you.

NATALYA PETROVNA. How do you know he's afraid of me?

VERA. He told me so.

NATALYA PETROVNA. Ah, he told you so! So he's more open with you than with others?

VERA. I don't know how he is with others, but with me he is . . . Perhaps it's because we're both orphans. Still, in his eyes, I'm just a child.

NATALYA PETROVNA. Do you think so? Of course I'm also very fond of him. He must have a very kind heart.

VERA. Oh, very, very kind! If only you knew how much everyone in the house loves him. He is so kind. He talks to everyone and is ready to help everyone. The day before yesterday he carried an old beggarwoman in his own arms right from the high road to the hospital. He once picked a flower for me so high up on a rock I had to close my eyes in fright. I thought he was bound to fall down and hurt himself . . . But he's so agile! You saw for yourself, down in the meadow yesterday evening, how agile he is.

NATALYA PETROVNA. Yes, that's true.

VERA. Remember how he ran after the kite and jumped over that ditch? All that's nothing to him.

NATALYA PETROVNA. Did he really pick a flower for you from a dangerous place? Clearly he loves you.

VERA [*after a pause*]. And he's always so happy . . . always so full of fun . . .

NATALYA PETROVNA. It's odd, though. Why is it in my presence . . .

VERA [*interrupting her*]. It's what I told you—he doesn't know you. But just wait, I'll tell him . . . I'll tell him there's no need to be afraid of you, is there? That you're so kind . . .

NATALYA PETROVNA [*with a forced laugh*]. Thank you.

VERA. You'll see. He'll listen to me, even though I am much younger than him.

NATALYA PETROVNA. I didn't know you were such friends with him. But do be careful, Vera. He is, of course, a splendid young man, but you know that at your age it won't do. People may start thinking . . . I remarked on this to you yesterday—remember?—in the garden. [*Vera lowers her eyes.*] On the other hand, I don't want to stand in the way of your affections, I'm only too sure of you and him . . . But still, you mustn't be angry with me, my dear, for being so pedantic. It is the job of us old people to bore the young by telling them what to do. In any case, I really don't need to say any of this because it's true, isn't it, that you like him and nothing more?

VERA [*shyly raising her eyes*]. He . . .

NATALYA PETROVNA. You see, you're looking at me as you did earlier, aren't you? Is that the way to look at a sister? Vera, listen, come close to me . . . [*Stroking her.*] What if your sister, your real, your very own sister, were right now to whisper in your ear the question: Vera, do you really not love anyone at all? Eh? What would you answer her? [*Vera glances indecisively at Natalya Petrovna.*] These pretty eyes of yours want to tell me something . . .

[*Vera suddenly presses her face to Natalya Petrovna's bosom. Natalya Petrovna goes pale and, after a momentary pause, continues.*] Are you in love? Tell me—are you?

VERA [*not raising her head*]. Oh, I don't know what's wrong with me . . .

NATALYA PETROVNA. Poor dear, you're in love! [*Vera presses herself more firmly still to Natalya Petrovna's bosom.*] You're in love . . . But is he, Vera, is he?

VERA [*still not raising her head*]. What're you asking me? I don't know . . . perhaps . . . I don't know, I don't know . . . [*Natalya Petrovna shivers and keeps very still. Vera raises her head and suddenly notices the change in her face.*] Natalya Petrovna, what's wrong?

NATALYA PETROVNA [*coming to herself*]. What's wrong? Nothing . . . nothing . . .

VERA. You're so pale, Natalya Petrovna, what's happened? Let me ring . . . [*Gets to her feet.*]

NATALYA PETROVNA. No, no, don't ring. It's nothing . . . it'll pass. There—it's gone already.

VERA. Let me at least go and call someone . . .

NATALYA PETROVNA. Quite the opposite, I'd like to . . . like to be alone. Listen, leave me, will you. We'll have another talk. Be off with you.

VERA. You're not angry with me, Natalya Petrovna, are you?

NATALYA PETROVNA. No, why should I be? Not in the least. On the contrary, I'm grateful to you for being so honest . . . Just leave me now, please. [*Vera tries to take her hand, but Natalya Petrovna turns away as if she had not seen Vera's gesture.*]

VERA [*with tears in her eyes*]. Natalya Petrovna . . .

NATALYA PETROVNA. Leave me, I beg you.

[*Exit Vera slowly into the study.*]

NATALYA PETROVNA [*alone, remaining for a short while quite still*]. Now I see it clearly—these children love each

other. [*Stops and draws her hand across her face.*] What of it?
So much the better! God grant them happiness! [*Laughing.*] And I . . . I could think . . . [*Again stops.*] She came
out with it so quickly, I confess I hadn't suspected, I
confess the news shocked me . . . But wait a moment,
everything's not over yet. My God, what am I saying?
What's wrong with me? I don't recognize myself, I don't
know what I've come to! [*A pause.*] What *have* I been
doing? I've been trying to marry the poor young girl—to
an old man! I send for the doctor, he insinuates this,
hints at that . . . Then there's Arkady and Rakitin . . .
And me . . . [*Gives a shudder and suddenly raises her head.*]
What's it all about after all? Am I jealous of Vera? I'm
really in love with him, am I? [*A pause.*] You can't go on
doubting it, can you? You are in love, you wretched
woman! I don't know how it happened. It's as if I'd been
given poison . . . Suddenly everything's gone to pieces,
scattered, done with . . . He's afraid of me . . . Everyone's
afraid of me. What am I to him? What's a creature like
me mean to him? He's young and she's young. And me!
[*Bitterly.*] How can he appreciate me? They're both of
them silly, as Rakitin says . . . Oh, how I hate that
clever-clever man! But Arkady, my trustful, kind Arkady!
My God, my God, I'd be better off dead! [*Stands up.*] I
think I'm going out of my mind. Oh, stop exaggerating!
Well—in a state of shock, then, astonished, amazed that
for the first time—yes, for the very first time—I'm in
love for the very first time in my life! [*She sits down again.*]
He must leave. Yes. And Rakitin too. The time's come
for me to sort myself out. I've gone down a notch—and
look where it's got me! And what on earth did I see in
him? [*After a moment's reflection.*] But it's frightful what
I'm feeling now . . . Arkady! Yes, I'll fling myself into his
arms, I'll beg him to forgive me, beg him to protect me
and save me, him and no one else! All the others are no
part of me and must remain like that. But surely . . .
surely there's another way? That girl—she's just a child.
She may be mistaken. It's all childishness anyhow . . .
Which means I'll—I'll have it out with him myself, I'll

ask him . . . [*Reproachfully.*] Ah, so you're still hoping, are you? You're still living in hope? Oh, what's the point of my hoping! My God, don't let me despise myself! [*Drops her head into her hands.*]

[*Enter Rakitin from the study, pale and anxious.*]

RAKITIN [*going up to Natalya Petrovna*]. Natalya Petrovna . . . [*She does not stir an inch. To himself:*] What on earth could have have happened between her and Vera? [*Loudly.*] Natalya Petrovna . . .

NATALYA PETROVNA [*raising her head*]. Who is it? Ah, it's you!

RAKITIN. Vera Aleksandrovna told me you weren't well . . . I . . .

NATALYA PETROVNA [*turning away*]. I'm quite well . . . Where could she have got the idea . . .

RAKITIN. No, Natalya Petrovna, you're not well. Just take one look at yourself.

NATALYA PETROVNA. Well, perhaps . . . But what's it to you? What do you want? Why are you here?

RAKITIN [*in a voice full of feeling*]. I'll tell you why I'm here. I came to ask your forgiveness. Half an hour ago I was unspeakably silly and rude to you . . . Forgive me. You see, Natalya Petrovna, no matter how modest a man's desires and . . . and hopes, he finds it hard not to lose control of himself for an instant when they are suddenly snatched from him. But now I've had time to reconsider, I've understood my position and why I'm at fault and I want only one thing—your forgiveness. [*He sits down quietly beside her.*] Look at me. Don't turn away. Here beside you is your old Rakitin, your friend, someone who doesn't demand anything more than permission to be a support for you, as you put it . . . Don't deny me your trust, do me a favour and forget that I ever . . . Forget anything that could have been hurtful . . .

NATALYA PETROVNA [*who has been staring all the time at the floor*]. Yes, yes . . . [*She stops.*] Oh, I'm sorry, Rakitin, I haven't heard a thing you said.

RAKITIN [*sadly*]. I was saying . . . I was asking for your forgiveness, Natalya Petrovna. I was asking you whether you would allow me to remain your friend.

NATALYA PETROVNA [*slowly turning towards him and placing both hands on his shoulders*]. Rakitin, tell me, what's wrong with me?

RAKITIN [*after a pause*]. You're in love.

NATALYA PETROVNA [*slowly repeating after him*]. I'm in love . . . But it's crazy, Rakitin, it's impossible. Surely it can't be so sudden . . . You say I'm in love . . . [*Falls silent.*]

RAKITIN. Yes, you're in love, poor woman. Don't deceive yourself.

NATALYA PETROVNA [*not looking at him*]. What can I do now?

RAKITIN. I'm ready to tell you, Natalya Petrovna, if you promise me . . .

NATALYA PETROVNA [*interrupting him and still not looking at him*]. You know that little girl, Vera, loves him . . . The two of them are in love.

RAKITIN. In that case it's all the more reason . . .

NATALYA PETROVNA [*again interrupts him*]. I've suspected it for a long time, but she's just now confessed everything . . . just now.

RAKITIN [*in a low voice, as if to himself*]. Poor woman!

NATALYA PETROVNA [*passing a hand across her face*]. Well, anyhow, it's time I took stock. I think you wanted to say something . . . Advise me what I should do, in God's name, Rakitin.

RAKITIN. I'm ready to advise you, Natalya Petrovna, only on one condition.

NATALYA PETROVNA. Tell me what it is.

RAKITIN. Promise you will not suspect my motives. Tell

me you're sure my desire to help you is quite unselfish. You can help me as well. Your faith in me will give me strength, or—better—allow me not to say a word.

NATALYA PETROVNA. Go on, go on.

RAKITIN. You don't doubt me?

NATALYA PETROVNA. Go on.

RAKITIN. Well, listen to this: he must go. [*Natalya Petrovna looks at him without speaking.*] Yes, he must go. I'm not going to talk to you about ... about your husband and about your duty. On my lips such words would be ... inappropriate. But these children love each other. You've just told me that yourself. Imagine if you came between them now—you'd be done for!

NATALYA PETROVNA. He must go ... [*After a pause.*] And you—will you be staying?

RAKITIN [*in confusion*]. I? ... I? [*After a pause.*] I must go as well. For the sake of your peace of mind, for your happiness and Verochka's, both he ... and I ... we must both go away for ever.

NATALYA PETROVNA. Rakitin ... I had sunk so low that I ... I was almost on the point of marrying off the poor girl, an orphan entrusted to me by my mother—to a silly, laughable old man! I simply didn't have the heart, Rakitin. The words literally died on my lips when she burst out laughing at my suggestion ... But I'd been having talks with that doctor, letting him smile at me knowingly. I'd put up with his smiles, his nods and winks ... Oh, I feel I'm on the edge of a precipice—please, please save me!

RAKITIN. Natalya Petrovna, you see I'm right. [*She says nothing. He goes on hurriedly.*] He must go ... We must both go. There's no other way out.

NATALYA PETROVNA [*dejectedly*]. What'll be the point of living then?

RAKITIN. My God, surely things haven't come to that ...

Natalya Petrovna, you'll recover, believe me. This'll all pass. What d'you mean—what'll be the point of living?

NATALYA PETROVNA. Yes, what'll be the point of living when you've all left me?

RAKITIN. But there's your family ... [*Natalya Petrovna lowers her eyes.*] Look, if you like, after he's gone I can stay on a few days ... just for ...

NATALYA PETROVNA [*sombrely*]. Ah, I see what you mean! For old times' sake, you're counting on our former friendship. You're hoping that I'll come to myself and return to you, isn't that it? I see what you mean.

RAKITIN [*reddening*]. Natalya Petrovna! How can you be so hurtful?

NATALYA PETROVNA [*bitterly*]. I see what you mean ... but you're fooling yourself.

RAKITIN. Why? After all your promises, after all I've been to you and you alone, for the sake of your happiness and your position in the world, finally ...

NATALYA PETROVNA. Ah, that's been a long-term concern of yours, has it? Why have you never mentioned this to me before?

RAKITIN [*rising*]. Natalya Petrovna, this very day, this very moment I'll leave here and you'll never see me again ... [*He makes as if to leave.*]

NATALYA PETROVNA [*holding out her arms to him*]. Michel, forgive me, I don't know what I'm saying ... You can see the position I'm in. Forgive me.

RAKITIN [*quickly returning to her and taking her by the hands*]. Natalya Petrovna ...

NATALYA PETROVNA. Oh, Michel, it's unutterably dreadful for me. [*She leans against his shoulder and presses a handkerchief to her eyes.*] Help me. I'll perish without you ...

[*At that moment the doors to the hall are flung open, and enter Islaev and Anna Semënovna.*]

ISLAEV [*loudly*]. I was always of the opinion . . .

[*He stops in astonishment at the sight of Rakitin and Natalya Petrovna. Natalya Petrovna glances round and exits in a hurry. Rakitin stays where he is, extremely embarrassed.*]

ISLAEV [*to Rakitin*]. What's the meaning of this? What's been going on?

RAKITIN. Nothing . . . it's . . .

ISLAEV. Is Natalya Petrovna unwell, is that it?

RAKITIN. No . . . but . . .

ISLAEV. So why's she suddenly run away? What were you two talking about? She seemed to be crying . . . Were you comforting her? What was it?

RAKITIN. Nothing really.

ANNA SEMËNOVNA. How could it be nothing, Mikhail Aleksandrych? [*After a pause.*] I'll go and see . . . [*She makes for the study.*]

RAKITIN [*stopping her*]. No, it'd be better if you left her alone, I beg you.

ISLAEV. What's all this mean? Tell me!

RAKITIN. Nothing, I assure you . . . Listen, I promise to explain everything to you today. I give you my word. But now, please, if you trust me, don't ask me anything—and don't disturb Natalya Petrovna.

ISLAEV. All right . . . only I'm astonished. This hasn't happened with Natasha before. It's quite unusual.

ANNA SEMËNOVNA. The chief thing is—what could have made Natasha cry? And what's she run away for—surely we're not strangers, are we?

RAKITIN. You mustn't say that—of course not! But listen, I've got to admit we didn't finish our talk. I must ask both of you just to let us have a little time alone.

ISLAEV. I see! There's a secret between you, is there?

RAKITIN. There is . . . but you'll find out what it is.

ISLAEV [*after a moment's thought*]. Let's go, mother, let's leave them alone. Then they can finish their mysterious talk.

ANNA SEMËNOVNA. But . . .

ISLAEV. Come on, come on. You heard him promise he'd explain everything.

RAKITIN. You can be certain . . .

ISLAEV [*coldly*]. Oh, I'm quite certain! [*To Anna Semënovna.*] Come on.

  [*Exit both.*]

RAKITIN [*watches them go and walks rapidly to the doors to the study*]. Natalya Petrovna . . . Natalya Petrovna, come out, I beg you.

NATALYA PETROVNA [*comes out of the study. She is very pale*]. What did they say?

RAKITIN. Nothing, don't worry . . . They were just a bit surprised. Your husband thought you were unwell. He saw how disturbed you were. Please sit down, you look so weak . . . [*Natalya Petrovna sits down.*] I told him . . . I asked him not to disturb us . . . to leave us alone.

NATALYA PETROVNA. And he agreed?

RAKITIN. Yes. I admit I had to promise him I'd explain everything tomorrow . . . Why did you go away?

NATALYA PETROVNA [*bitterly*]. You ask why . . . But what'll you tell him?

RAKITIN. I . . . I'll think of something. But that needn't concern us now. We've got to make the most of this chance to talk. You see it can't go on . . . You're not in any state to endure excitements of this kind . . . And they're unworthy of you . . . I myself . . . But that's beside the point. You simply must be firm—I can look after myself! Look, you agree with me, don't you?

NATALYA PETROVNA. About what?

RAKITIN. About the need . . . for us to leave. You agree, don't you? One can't shilly-shally at a time like this. If you'll allow me, I'll myself talk to Belyaev at once. He's a good chap, he'll understand . . .

NATALYA PETROVNA. You intend to talk to him—you? But what on earth can you say to him?

RAKITIN [*in confusion*]. I . . .

NATALYA PETROVNA [*after a pause*]. Rakitin, look, doesn't it seem to you that we're both crazy? I got scared and scared you and perhaps it's all nonsense.

RAKITIN. How?

NATALYA PETROVNA. I mean it. What's happened to the two of us? I think everything used to be so calm, so quiet, in this house—and suddenly it's all got out of hand! I mean we've all gone out of our minds. Enough, then, let's stop playing the fool, let's start living the way we used to . . . And there won't be any need for you to explain anything to Arkady. I'll tell him myself what we've been up to and the two of us can have a good laugh about it. My husband and I don't need a go-between!

RAKITIN. Natalya Petrovna, you really scare me at this moment. You're smiling and yet you're pale as death. Just remember what you said to me only a quarter of an hour ago . . .

NATALYA PETROVNA. Oh, that's nothing! However, I see what's the matter—you're stirring up a storm yourself so at least you won't be the only one to drown!

RAKITIN. Once again suspicions, once again reproaches, Natalya Petrovna . . . God help you, but you're putting me through it. Or are you regretting your frankness?

NATALYA PETROVNA. I don't regret anything.

RAKITIN. How am I to take that?

NATALYA PETROVNA [*animatedly*]. Rakitin, if you say a single word on my behalf or about me to Belyaev, I'll never forgive you.

RAKITIN. Aha, so that's it! Don't worry, Natalya Petrovna. I not only won't say a word to Mr Belyaev, but I won't even say goodbye to him, when I leave here. I don't intend to foist myself on anyone.

NATALYA PETROVNA [*in some confusion*]. Perhaps you think I've changed my opinion about, er . . . about his going away?

RAKITIN. I don't think anything.

NATALYA PETROVNA. On the contrary, I am so convinced of the need for him to leave, as you put it, that I intend to dismiss him myself. [*A short pause.*] Yes, I'll tell him myself.

RAKITIN. You will?

NATALYA PETROVNA. Yes, I will. Rightaway. I ask you to send him to me.

RAKITIN. What—now?

NATALYA PETROVNA. Right now. I beg you, Rakitin. You can see I am completely calm. Besides, they won't interrupt me now. I've got to make the most of this opportunity . . . I'll be very grateful to you. I'll just ask him a few things . . .

RAKITIN. For heaven's sake, he won't tell you anything. He himself told me he felt awkward in your presence.

NATALYA PETROVNA [*suspiciously*]. Ah, so you've already spoken to him about me, have you? [*Rakitin shrugs.*] Well, forgive me, forgive me, Michel, and just send him to me. You'll see that I'll dismiss him and everything'll be done with. It will all be over and forgotten like a bad dream. Please send him. It is absolutely essential I talk things out with him once and for all. You'll be quite content with me. Please.

RAKITIN [*who has had his gaze fixed on her the whole time, coldly and sadly*]. Certainly. Your wish is my command. [*Goes towards the hall doors.*]

NATALYA PETROVNA [*to him as he goes*]. Thank you very much, Michel.

RAKITIN [*turning round*]. Oh, don't thank me—not in the very least! [*Exits rapidly into the hall.*]

NATALYA PETROVNA [*on her own, after a pause*]. He's a

good, decent man. But was I ever in love with him?
[*Stands up.*] He is right, the young man must go. But how
can I just dismiss him? I simply want to know whether
he's fond of that girl. Perhaps it's all nonsense. How
could I have got myself so worked up? Why have I been
saying all these things? Well, there's nothing to be done
about that now. I want to know what he'll say. But he
must go . . . definitely . . . definitely. Perhaps he won't
want to say anything—after all, he's afraid of me, isn't
he? So what! So much the better! We haven't got a lot to
talk about . . . [*Presses her hand to her temples.*] My head
aches. Shall I put it off till tomorrow? Shall I? Today I
get the impression everyone's watching me . . . Oh, what
have I come to! No, it'd be better to get it over with once
and for all! One last try and I'll be free! Oh, how I long
for freedom and peace of mind!* [*Belyaev enters from the
hall.*] It's him!

BELYAEV [*going up to her*]. Natalya Petrovna, Mikhailo
Aleksandrych says you'd like to see me . . .

NATALYA PETROVNA [*with an effort*]. Yes, that's true. I've
got to . . . to get things straight with you.

BELYAEV. Get things straight?

NATALYA PETROVNA [*without looking at him*]. Ye-e-s . . .
[*After a pause.*] Permit me to tell you, Aleksei Nikolaich,
that I'm . . . I'm not satisfied with you.

BELYAEV. May I ask for what reason?

NATALYA PETROVNA. Please listen to me. I, er, I don't
quite know where to begin. Still, I should warn you that
my dissatisfaction is not the result of any negligence on
your part. On the contrary, I am pleased by the way you
have been getting on with Kolya.

BELYAEV. Then what can it be?

NATALYA PETROVNA [*glancing at him*]. You needn't be
alarmed—your sin is not all that great. You're young.
You've probably never lived in a strange house. You
couldn't foresee . . .

BELYAEV. But, Natalya Petrovna . . .

NATALYA PETROVNA. You want to know what it's all about, don't you? I understand your impatience. So I must tell you that Verochka . . . [*Giving him a glance.*] . . . Verochka has confessed to me everything.

BELYAEV [*in astonishment*]. Vera Aleksandrovna? What could Vera Aleksandrovna confess to you? And what have I got to do with with it?

NATALYA PETROVNA. You really don't know what she could confess? You can't guess?

BELYAEV. Not in the slightest.

NATALYA PETROVNA. In that case, forgive me. If you really can't guess, then I owe you an apology. I think . . . I think I may have been mistaken. But let me say that I don't believe you. I understand what may have made you say it . . . I have great respect for your modesty.

BELYAEV. I really do not understand you, Natalya Petrovna.

NATALYA PETROVNA. Really and truly? You mean you are trying to assure me that you haven't noticed what the child's feelings for you are, what Vera feels for you?

BELYAEV. Vera Aleksandrovna's feeling for me? I don't even know what to say about that—for pity's sake! I think I've always treated Vera Aleksandrovna the same as . . .

NATALYA PETROVNA. As everyone else, you mean? [*After a short silence.*] Whether that's true nor not, whether you really don't know or whether you're pretending, the fact is—the girl's in love with you. She herself confessed it. Well, now I am asking you, as an honourable man, what do you intend to do about it?

BELYAEV [*in confusion*]. What do I intend to do about it?

NATALYA PETROVNA [*crossing her arms*]. Yes.

BELYAEV. This is all so unexpected, Natalya Petrovna . . .

NATALYA PETROVNA [*after a pause*]. Aleksei Nikolaich, I

see . . . I see I've handled this wrongly. You don't understand me. You imagine I'm angry with you . . . but I'm only . . . only a bit upset. And that's very natural. Please don't be alarmed. Let's sit down. [*They both sit.*] I will be frank with you, Aleksei Nikolaich, and you should be just a little bit more trusting towards me. You really don't have to be afraid of me. Vera is in love with you . . . Of course you're not to blame for this. I am prepared to suppose that you're not responsible . . . But you see, don't you, Aleksei Nikolaich, she's an orphan and I'm in charge of her, I have to answer for her, for her future, for her happiness. She is still young and I am sure that the feeling which you have aroused in her can quickly vanish away—at her age love can be short-lived. But you understand that it was my duty to warn you. It is always dangerous to play with fire . . . And I don't doubt that now you know her feeling for you you will change your attitude to her, you will avoid seeing her and going out for walks . . . I'm right, aren't I? I can rely on you. With someone else I would have been frightened of being so direct.

BELYAEV. Natalya Petrovna, believe me, I can appreciate . . .

NATALYA PETROVNA. I am telling you that I don't doubt you. In any case, this will all remain a secret between us.

BELYAEV. I confess to you, Natalya Petrovna, I find everything you've said to me so strange . . . Of course I don't dare disbelieve you, but . . .

NATALYA PETROVNA. Look, Aleksei Nikolaich, everything I've said to you now I've said on the assumption that on your part—there is nothing in it . . . [*She interrupts herself.*] Because if this were not the case . . . of course, I still don't know you that well, but I know enough about you to see no reason to stand in the way of your intentions. You're not rich—but you're young, you have a future ahead of you, and when two people love each other . . . I say to you again I considered it my duty to warn you as an honourable man about the consequences of your friendship with Vera, but if you . . .

BELYAEV [*in some bewilderment*]. I really don't know, Natalya Petrovna, what you mean . . .

NATALYA PETROVNA [*hurriedly*]. Oh, you must believe me, I'm not asking for a confession from you, I can do without that . . . I can see from your behaviour what it's all about . . . [*Glancing at him.*] However, I must tell you that Vera thought you were not completely indifferent to her.

BELYAEV [*after a pause stands up*]. Natalya Petrovna, I see that I can't stay any longer in your house.

NATALYA PETROVNA [*flaring up*]. I think you might have waited until I had dismissed you . . . [*Stands up.*]

BELYAEV. You have been frank with me, allow me to be frank with you. I do not love Vera Aleksandrovna. At least I do not love her in the way you suppose.

NATALYA PETROVNA. Surely you don't think I . . . [*Stops.*]

BELYAEV. If Vera Aleksandrovna has taken a liking to me, if, as you say, she is not indifferent to me, I do not want to deceive her—I'll tell her everything myself, the whole truth. But after such plain speaking you will yourself understand, Natalya Petrovna, that it'll be hard for me to stay here. My position would be too awkward. I won't try telling you how difficult it'll be for me to leave your house, but I've got no choice. I will always think of you with gratitude . . . Allow me to go now. I will say goodbye to you later.

NATALYA PETROVNA [*with pretend indifference*]. As you wish. But I confess I hadn't expected this. This wasn't the reason why I wanted to have a talk with you. I simply wanted to warn you—Vera's still a child . . . Perhaps I've ascribed too much significance to it. However, it's as you wish.

BELYAEV. Natalya Petrovna, I really can't stay here any longer.

NATALYA PETROVNA. You evidently find it very easy to leave us!

BELYAEV. No. Natalya Petrovna, I don't find it easy.

NATALYA PETROVNA. I'm not accustomed to detaining people against their will but . . . but I confess I find this very unpleasant.

BELYAEV [*after some uncertainty*]. Natalya Petrovna . . . I haven't wanted to cause you the least unpleasantness . . . I will stay.

NATALYA PETROVNA [*suspiciously*]. Ah! [*After a pause.*] I hadn't expected you to change your mind so quickly. I'm grateful to you but . . . but let me think. Perhaps you're right, perhaps you ought to go. I'll think about it and let you know. Will you allow me to leave you in ignorance until this evening?

BELYAEV. I'm ready to wait as long as you like. [*Bows and intends to leave.*]

NATALYA PETROVNA. Promise me one thing . . .

BELYAEV [*stopping*]. What, ma'am?

NATALYA PETROVNA. I think you wanted to speak to Vera. I don't think that would be proper. However, I'll let you know my decision. I'm beginning to think that you ought to go. Goodbye for the time being.

[*Belyaev bows a second time and exits into the hall. Natalya Petrovna watches him go.*]

I don't need to worry! He doesn't love her! [*Walks about the room.*] So instead of dismissing him, I'm keeping him here, am I? He'll be staying . . . But what'll I tell Rakitin? What have I done? [*After a pause.*] And what right did I have to broadcast the news of that poor child being in love? Why did I? I myself wormed the confession out of her—or the semi-confession, and then I cruelly and crudely . . . [*Covers her face with her hands.*] Perhaps he's begun to fall in love with her . . . What right did I have to trample on this little flower at the outset? Oh, enough of that—have I trampled on it, or perhaps he's misled me? I certainly wanted to mislead *him*! Oh, no, he's much too honourable, he's not like me! Why was I in such a hurry? Why have I chattered so much about it all? [*Sighs.*] Well, enough's enough! If only I could have foreseen . . . Oh, how I pretended, how I lied to him! And he—how boldly and freely he spoke! I just grovel before him, he's a real man! I didn't know what he was really like—Still, he must go. If he stays, I feel I'll reach the point when I lose all self-respect. He must go or I'm done for! I'll write to him before he's had time to see Vera . . . He *must* go! [*Exits swiftly into the study.*]

ACT FOUR

The scene is a large, empty vestibule. The walls are bare, the floor of uneven stone. Six brick columns, whitewashed and peeling, support the ceiling, three on each side. On the left are two open windows and a door into the garden. On the right is a door into the corridor leading to the main house. Centre is an iron door to a store-room. Beside the first column on the right is a green garden bench. In one corner stand several spades, watering-cans and pots. The time is evening. Red sunset rays fall from the windows on to the floor.

KATYA [*entering from the door on the right, going quickly to a window and looking out into the garden for a moment or so*]. No, he's not to be seen. They said he'd gone to the conservatory. It means he's not yet come out. So I'll wait till he comes past. There isn't any other way . . . [*Sighs and leans against the window.*] I've heard he's leavin'. [*Again sighs.*] What'll we do when he's gone . . . Oh, the poor young lady! How she begged me . . . Well, why shouldn't I do her a good turn? Let 'im have a talk to her before he goes. Ooh, it's hot today! And, look, it's rainin'! [*Again looks out of the window and suddenly draws back.*] What're they doin' 'ere? They're comin' this way! Ooh, lordy, lordy! [*Tries to run away, but does not reach the door into the corridor in time before Shpigelsky and Lizaveta Bogdanovna enter from the garden. Katya hides behind a column.*]

SHPIGELSKY [*shaking his cap*]. We can wait here for the shower to pass. It'll soon be over.

LIZAVETA BOGDANOVNA. Let's do that.

SHPIGELSKY [*looking round*]. What sort of place is this? A store-room?

LIZAVETA BOGDANOVNA [*pointing to the iron door*]. No,

the store-room's there. They say it's a vestibule Arkady Sergeich had built when he came back from abroad.

SHPIGELSKY. Ah, I see now—Venice, my dear sir, Venice! [*Sits down on the bench.*] Let's sit down. [*Lizaveta Bogdanovna sits down.*] You've got to admit, Lizaveta Bogdanovna, that shower came at the wrong moment. It interrupted our *tête-à-tête* at a very sensitive point.

LIZAVETA BOGDANOVNA [*lowering her eyes*]. Ignaty Ilich . . .

SHPIGELSKY. But no one is going to stop us renewing our conversation . . . By the way, did you say Anna Semënovna was out of sorts today?

LIZAVETA BOGDANOVNA. Yes, she's out of sorts. She even had her food in her own room.

SHPIGELSKY. Well I never! Things *are* bad, just imagine!

LIZAVETA BOGDANOVNA. This morning she found Natalya Petrovna in tears . . . with Mikhailo Aleksandrych. Of course, he's a family friend, but still . . . However, Mikhailo Aleksandrych has promised to explain everything.

SHPIGELSKY. Ah! Well, she's no reason to be alarmed. Mikhailo Aleksandrych was never a dangerous man, to my mind, and he's a great deal less dangerous now than he was.

LIZAVETA BOGDANOVNA. How do you mean?

SHPIGELSKY. I mean what I say. He's very infectious with words. Some come out in a rash, but clever people like him come out in chatter, they infect you with their tongue. You, Lizaveta Bogdanovna, needn't be frightened of talkers—they're not dangerous. It's the ones who keep quiet, and the dotty ones, and the very temperamental ones, and the ones with thick necks—they're the real danger.

LIZAVETA BOGDANOVNA [*after a pause*]. Tell me, is Natalya Petrovna really unwell?

SHPIGELSKY. Just as unwell as you and I are.

LIZAVETA BOGDANOVNA. At dinner she didn't eat a thing.

SHPIGELSKY. It's not only illness that takes away appetite.

LIZAVETA BOGDANOVNA. Did you have dinner at Bolshintsov's?

SHPIGELSKY. Yes, I did. I went over to see him. And I came back here just to see you, cross my heart!

LIZAVETA BOGDANOVNA. Oh, do stop it! But you know something, Ignaty Ilich, Natalya Petrovna's got it in for you . . . At dinner she wasn't at all flattering about you.

SHPIGELSKY. Really? Clearly ladies don't find it to their taste when people of my sort have sharp eyes. You've got to do what they ask, help them, and then pretend you don't understand what they're up to—that's what they're like! Well, let's wait and see. And Rakitin was down in the dumps, I imagine?

LIZAVETA BOGDANOVNA. Yes, he also seemed not quite himself today.

SHPIGELSKY. Hmm. And Vera Alexandrovna? And Belyaev?

LIZAVETA BOGDANOVNA. They all seemed quite out of sorts. I really can't think what's happened to everyone today.

SHPIGELSKY. The more you learn, the older you'll get, Lizaveta Bogdanovna . . . Well, that's enough about them. Let's talk about us. As you can see, the rain's not over yet . . . Would you like that?

LIZAVETA BOGDANOVNA [affectedly lowering her eyes]. What are you asking me, Ignaty Ilich?

SHPIGELSKY. Oh, Liza Bogdanovna, may I ask—why all this fluttering of the eyes, all this show of false modesty? We're not young things, you and I! Giving oneself airs, paying compliments, uttering sighs—they're not for us. Let's talk calmly and in a businesslike way as befits people of our years. So the question is—we're fond of one another . . . at least I'm presuming you're fond of me . . .

LIZAVETA BOGDANOVNA [*in a slightly affected way*]. Really, Ignaty Ilich . . .

SHPIGELSKY. All right, all right. As a woman you're bound to, you know . . . [*Demonstrates with his hand.*] . . . Bound to be a wee bit circumspect. Anyhow—we're fond of each other. And in other respects we're much of a muchness. For my own part I must say that I have no claim to noble antecedents, nor do you. I'm not a rich man; if I were I'd not . . . [*Laughs.*] But I've got a decent practice and not all my patients die. According to you, you have fifteen thousand roubles' worth of private capital. All of which is not bad, as you can see. In addition, I imagine you're bored with being nothing but a governess and looking after an old woman, playing *préférence* with her and dancing attendance on her—there can't be much joy in that. For my part, it's not so much that I'm bored with my bachelor life, but I'm getting old—and my cooks are all stealing from me. Anyhow, everything's as it should be, if you know what I mean. But the difficulty is, Lizaveta Bogdanovna, we scarcely know each other at all—or, truth to tell, you don't know me, but I *do* know you. I know what sort of person you are. I won't say you haven't developed certain foibles. Being an old maid, you've gone a bit sour—but there's nothing bad in that. A wife is wax in a good husband's hands. But I'd like you to get to know me before we are married, otherwise you may hold things against me afterwards . . . I don't want to deceive you.

LIZAVETA BOGDANOVNA [*with dignity*]. But, Ignaty Ilich, I think I've also had occasion to get to know what sort of person you are . . .

SHPIGELSKY. You have? Oh, stop it—that's not a woman's business. You probably think, don't you, that I'm a man of happy disposition, a jolly fellow, eh?

LIZAVETA BOGDANOVNA. It's always seemed to me you you were a very cordial man . . .

SHPIGELSKY. There you are, you see! It's easy to be

mistaken. Because I always play the fool in front of
strangers, telling them jokes and playing up to them,
you've come to the conclusion that I'm really a happy,
cordial man. If it weren't that I needed them, these
strangers, I wouldn't bother to glance at them ... Still,
whenever I can, you know, without great danger, I poke
fun at them ... However, I'm not fooling myself, I know
there are certain ladies and gentlemen who need me at
every turn and are bored stiff without me who still feel
they've the right to despise me. In that case I don't feel I
owe them a thing. Take Natalya Petrovna ... Do you
think I don't see her through and through? [*Imitating
her.*] 'My dear doctor, I really am very fond of you—
you've got the wickedest tongue ...' Ha! Ha! Ha! coo
away, my little dove, coo away! Oh, these grand miladies!
The way they smile at you and make little eyes at you—
you know what I mean?—and yet they've got aversion
written all over their faces! They really can't stand you—
and you can't do a thing about it! I know why she wasn't
at all flattering about me today. They really are astonishing, these grand miladies! Because they splash themselves with eau-de-Cologne every day and speak in such
a casual drawl just as if they were dropping the words
one by one and expecting you to pick them up, they
imagine they'll never get caught out. It ain't like that!
They're just mortals like the rest of us poor sinners!

LIZAVETA BOGDANOVNA. Ignaty Ilich, you astonish me!

SHPIGELSKY. I knew I'd astonish you. You are beginning
to see that I'm not a jolly fellow at all, perhaps not even
all that kind ... But I also don't want to pretend to you
that I am what I've never been. No matter how much I
fawn before these ladies and gents, no one's ever made a
fool of me and no one's ever led me by the nose. I can
even say they're a bit frightened of me. They know I can
bite. Once upon a time, about three years ago, at dinner,
a certain gent, a real yokel, stuck a radish in my hair for
the fun of it. What do you think I did, eh? That very
instant—coolly, mind, and very politely—I challenged

him to a duel. The fellow was almost paralysed with fear. My host forced him to apologize—the effect was quite extraordinary! I confess I knew beforehand he wouldn't fight. So you see, Lizaveta Bogdanovna, I am inordinately vain—and that's the way my life has worked out! I'm not a man of many talents, just picked things up any old how. I'm a bad doctor, there's no point in hiding that from you, and if you fall ill I won't be the one to treat you. If I'd had any talent and education, I'd have gone off to St Petersburg. Still, for the people round here, of course, there's no need for a better doctor. As for my own character, I must warn you, Lizaveta Bogdanovna, that at home I'm gloomy, taciturn and demanding; I keep my temper usually when I'm looked after and pampered; I love it when all my little habits are catered for and I'm given tasty food. However, I am not jealous and I am not mean, and when I'm away you can do just what you like. Of so-called romantic love between us, you understand, not a word need be said. However, I imagine it's still possible to live with me under the same roof . . . provided I'm indulged and no one starts crying in my presence—I can't stand tears! I am not a nagger. There you have it—my confession. Well, what'll you say now?

LIZAVETA BOGDANOVNA. What *can* I say, Ignaty Ilich? If you hadn't intentionally blackened yourself . . .

SHPIGELSKY. Blackened myself—how? You mustn't forget that someone else in my place might have quite calmly not breathed a word about his faults, hoping you wouldn't notice, but after marriage—then he'd have started playing up—and after marriage it would have been too late. But I am too proud for that. [*Lizaveta Bogdanovna looks at him.*] Yes, yes, I'm too proud . . . You don't need to look at me like that. I don't intend to lie or pretend to my future wife, not for fifteen thousand roubles or a hundred thousand. But to a stranger I can be politeness itself for a sack of flour. That's the sort of man I am . . . I can be all smiles to a stranger while all the time thinking: Eh, you blockhead, I'll soon have you hooked! But with you I say what I think. That is to say, if you'll permit me, I don't tell you everything I think, but at least I don't pretend to you. I must seem to you a mighty odd fellow, that's for sure, but just you wait, sometime I'll tell you the story of my life and you'll be astonished how I've survived. Probably you didn't eat off gold plate when you were a child, but still, my dear, you can't imagine what real, grinding proverty is . . . However, I'll tell you all about that another time. But now you'd better think over what I've had the honour to tell you. Consider it carefully, on your own, and let me know your decision. So far as I can judge, you're a woman of common sense. You're . . . By the way, how old are you?

LIZAVETA BOGDANOVNA. I'm . . . I'm . . . thirty.

SHPIGELSKY [*calmly*]. That's a lie, you're all of forty.

LIZAVETA BOGDANOVNA [*flaring up*]. I am not forty, but thirty-six.

SHPIGELSKY. It's still not thirty. You must get out of the habit of saying that sort of thing, Lizaveta Bogdanovna, more especially as a married woman of thirty-six is certainly not old. You also ought to stop taking snuff. [*Stands up.*] I think the shower's over.

LIZAVETA BOGDANOVNA [*also standing up*]. Yes, it is.

SHPIGELSKY. So you'll give me an answer in a few days?

LIZAVETA BOGDANOVNA. I will let you know my decision tomorrow.

SHPIGELSKY. That's what I like! That's sensible, so sensible! Ah, Lizaveta Bogdanovna, give me your arm! Let's go to the house.

LIZAVETA BOGDANOVNA [*giving him her arm*]. Yes, let's be off.

SHPIGELSKY. Oh, by the way, I haven't kissed you yet— and I think it's the done thing . . . Well, here goes! [*Kisses her hand. Lizaveta Bogdanovna blushes.*] There. [*Moves towards the door into the garden.*]

LIZAVETA BOGDANOVNA [*stopping*]. So you think, Ignaty Ilich, that Mikhailo Aleksandrych isn't dangerous?

SHPIGELSKY. That's what I think.

LIZAVETA BOGDANOVNA. Do you know something, Ignaty Ilich, I think for some time Natalya Petrovna's . . . I think Mr Belyaev . . . Don't you think she pays a lot of attention to him? And Verochka, what do you think about her? Isn't that why today she's . . .

SHPIGELSKY [*interrupting her*]. I forgot to tell you one thing, Lizaveta Bogdanovna. I am myself frightfully inquisitive, but I can't stand inquisitive women. Let me explain: in my opinion, a wife should be inquisitive and observant—that can even be a very useful thing for a husband—but only so far as *other people* are concerned. You understand me: other people. However, if you really want to know my opinion about Natalya Petrovna, Vera Aleksandrovna, Mr Belyaev and all the local inhabitants, listen a moment and I'll sing you a song. I've got a dreadful voice, so don't complain.

LIZAVETA BOGDANOVNA [*in astonishment*]. A song?

SHPIGELSKY. Listen. Here's the first verse:

> Grandma had a little grey goat,*
> Grandma had a little grey goat,
> What a little grey goat, it was, it was!
> What a pretty little grey goat!

The second verse goes:

> The little grey goat went into the wood,
> The little grey goat went into the wood,
> Into the wood it went, it went!
> Into the wood went the little grey goat!

LIZAVETA BOGDANOVNA. But I really don't understand . . .

SHPIGELSKY. Listen. The third verse goes:

> Big bad wolves ate up the goat,
> Big bad wolves ate up the goat. [*Jumps about.*]
> They ate it right up, they did, they did!
> They ate up grandma's pretty grey goat!

And now let's go. In any case, I've got to have a word
with Natalya Petrovna. Hopefully she won't bite. If I'm
not mistaken she still needs me. Let's go.

[*They exit into the garden.*]

KATYA [*emerging cautiously from behind a pillar*]. At last
they've gone! What a wicked tongue that doctor's got—
talk, talk, talk! An' doesn't he sing something awful?
I'm frightened Aleksei Nikolaich may have gone back
to the house in the meantime ... They didn't have to
come here, did they? [*Goes to the window.*] So Lizaveta
Bogdanovna'll be the doctor's wife, will she? [*Laughs.*]
Well I never! I don't envy her ... [*Looks out of the
window.*] How wonderfully fresh and washed the grass
looks! What a lovely smell! It's the cherry blossom ...
Oh, there he is! [*After a pause.*] Aleksei Nikolaich!
Aleksei Nikolaich!

BELYAEV'S VOICE [*offstage*]. Who's calling? Ah, is it you,
Katya? [*Comes to the window.*] What do you want?

KATYA. Come in here. I've got something to tell you.

BELYAEV. Oh, all right. [*Leaves the window and in a moment
appears in the doorway.*] Here I am.

KATYA. Did you get wet in the rain?

BELYAEV. No. I was sitting in the greenhouse with Potap.
He's your uncle, isn't he?

KATYA. Yes, sir, he's my uncle.

BELYAEV. How pretty you're looking today! [*Katya smiles
and lowers her eyes. He takes a peach out of his pocket.*] Would
you like it?

KATYA [*indicating refusal*]. Thank you very much—you
have it.

BELYAEV. Did I say no when you offered me raspberries
yesterday? Take it. I picked it for you—really.

KATYA. Well, thank you very much. [*Takes the peach.*]

BELYAEV. Right. So what was it you wanted to tell me?

KATYA. The young lady, Vera Aleksandrovna, begged me to tell you she, er, wants to see you.

BELYAEV. Oh, well, I'll go and see her at once.

KATYA. No, sir. She, er, she'll be comin' 'ere. She's got to talk to you.

BELYAEV [*in some astonishment*]. She wants to come *here*?

KATYA. Yes, sir. Here, you know—nobody comes here, so you won't be interrupted. [*Sighs.*] She's very much in love with you, Aleksei Nikolaich, an' . . . an' she is such a kind girl. I'll go an' fetch her, shall I? An' you'll wait here?

BELYAEV. Of course, of course.

KATYA. One moment . . . [*Goes and then stops*]. Aleksei Nikolaich, is it true what they say—that you're leaving?

BELYAEV. Me? No. Who told you that?

KATYA. So you're not going? Oh, thank God! [*In some confusion.*] We'll be back in a moment. [*Exits through the door leading to the house.*]

BELYAEV [*remaining motionless for a short time*]. Wonders'll never cease! They seem to be happening to me. I confess I'd not expected all this—Vera in love with me, Natalya Petrovna knowing it, Vera admitting it . . . Wonders'll never cease! Vera's such a dear, kind child, but . . . but what's this note mean, for instance? [*Takes a small scrap of paper out of his pocket.*] It's from Natalya Petrovna in pencil: 'Don't leave, don't make any decision until I've spoken to you.' But what's she want to talk to me about? [*Pauses.*] I'm having the silliest ideas! I find it all extremely embarrassing. If someone had told me a month ago that I'd . . . I'd . . . I can't really get over that conversation with Natalya Petrovna. Why's my heart beating like this? And now Vera wants to see me . . . What'll I say to her? At least I'll learn what it's all about . . . Perhaps Natalya Petrovna's annoyed with me. But why? [*Studies the note again.*] It's all strange, very strange. [*The door opens quietly. He quickly puts away the note. Enter*

Vera and Katya. He goes up to them. Vera is very pale, keeps her eyes lowered and remains in the doorway.]

KATYA. Don't be frightened, miss, you go up to him. I'll keep watch. Don't be frightened. [*To Belyaev.*] Oh, Aleksei Nikolaich! [*She closes the windows, exits into the garden and locks the door behind her.*]

BELYAEV. Vera Aleksandrovna, you wanted to see me. Come here and sit down. [*Takes her by the hand and leads her to the bench. Vera sits down.*] That's right. [*Looking at her with surprise.*] Have you been crying?

VERA [*not raising her eyes*]. It's nothing . . . I came here to ask you to forgive me, Aleksei Nikolaich.

BELYAEV. For what?

VERA. I heard . . . I heard you'd had an unpleasant talk with Natalya Petrovna . . . and you're leaving, you've been dismissed.

BELYAEV. Who told you this?

VERA. Natalya Petrovna herself. I saw her after her talk with you. She told me you yourself didn't want to stay here any longer. But I think you've been dismissed.

BELYAEV. Tell me—do they all know about this in the house?

VERA. No, just Katya. I had to tell her. I wanted to talk to you and ask you to forgive me. Imagine how difficult everything is for me now . . . I mean, I'm the cause of it all, I'm the one who's to blame.

BELYAEV. You are, Vera Aleksandrovna?

VERA. I couldn't have expected—I mean, Natalya Petrovna . . . Anyhow I don't blame her. You mustn't blame me, too. This morning I was a silly child, but now . . . [*Stops.*]

BELYAEV. Nothing's settled yet, Vera Aleksandrovna. I may be staying.

VERA [*sadly*]. You say nothing's settled, Aleksei Nikolaich—no, it's all settled, it's all over. Look at the two of us now—and just remember what it was like yesterday in the garden. [*A pause.*] Oh, I can see Natalya Petrovna's told you everything.

BELYAEV [*in some confusion*]. Vera Aleksandrovna . . .

VERA. I can see she's told you everything . . . She wanted to trap me and like a fool I ran straight into it. But she gave herself away, too. I'm not as much of a child as all that. [*Lowering her voice.*] Oh, no, I'm not!

BELYAEV. What exactly do you mean?

VERA [*glancing at him*]. Aleksei Nikolaich, is it true you wanted to leave?

BELYAEV. Yes.

VERA. Why? [*Belyaev says nothing.*] Why don't you answer me?

BELYAEV. Vera Aleksandrovna, you were right—Natalya Petrovna told me everything.

VERA [*in a weak voice*]. What, for instance?

BELYAEV. Vera Aleksandrovna . . . I really can't . . . You know what I mean.

VERA. Perhaps she told you that I was in love with you?

BELYAEV [*indecisively*]. Yes.

VERA [*rapidly*]. It isn't true.

BELYAEV [*in confusion*]. What?

VERA [*covering her face with her hands and whispering hollow-voiced through her fingers*]. At least I never said that to her, though I don't remember . . . [*Raising her head.*] Oh, she's treated me so cruelly! And you . . . you want to leave because of this?

BELYAEV. Vera Aleksandrovna, judge for yourself . . .

VERA [*glancing at him*]. He doesn't love me! [*Again covers her face.*]

BELYAEV [*sits down beside her and takes her hand*]. Vera Aleksandrovna, give me your hand . . . Look, we mustn't have any misunderstandings. I love you like a sister. I

love you because it's impossible not to. Forgive me if I
... In my entire life I was never in a position like this
... I wouldn't want to insult you ... I won't try to
pretend to you—I know you liked me, you fell in love
with me ... But judge for yourself: what'll come out of
it? I'm only twenty and I haven't got a penny. Please
don' get mad with me. I really don't know what to say to
you.

VERA [*taking her hands away from her face and looking at him*].
As if I were demanding anything of you, my God! But
why be so cruel, why be so hard-hearted ... [*She stops.*]

BELYAEV. Vera Aleksandrovna, I didn't want to hurt you.

VERA. I'm not blaming you, Aleksei Nikolaich. You're not
to blame. I'm the only one to blame! And that's why I'm
being punished! And I don't blame her. I know she's a
kind woman, but she couldn't get the better of herself ...
She lost control.

BELYAEV [*bewildered*]. She lost control?

VERA[*turning to him*]. Natalya Petrovna's in love with you,
Belyaev.

BELYAEV. What?

VERA. She's in love with you.

BELYAEV. What are you saying?

VERA. I know what I'm saying. I've grown up a lot today.
I'm not a child any more, believe me. She took it into
her head ... to be jealous of me! [*With a bitter smile.*]
What do you think of that?

BELYAEV. It's impossible!

VERA. Impossible ... Then why did she suddenly make
up her mind to marry me off to that what's-his-name—
Bolshintsov? Why was she sending the doctor to talk to
me, why was she trying to persuade me herself? Oh, I
know what I'm saying all right! If only you could have
seen, Belyaev, the way her face changed when I told her!
Oh, you can't imagine how sly she was, how cleverly she

wormed the confession out of me . . . Yes, she's in love with you, it's all too obvious . . .

BELYAEV. Vera Aleksandrovna, you're wrong, I assure you.

VERA. No, I'm not wrong. Believe me—I'm not wrong. If she isn't in love with you, why's she been so cruel to me? What have I done to her? [*Bitterly.*] Jealousy's to blame. There's nothing more to be said! And look—why's she dismissed you? She thinks you . . . you and I . . . Oh, she doesn't have to worry! And you can stay! [*Covers her face with her hands.*]

BELYAEV. She hasn't dismissed me so far. As I told you, nothing's decided yet . . .

VERA [*suddenly raising her head and looking at him*]. Really?

BELYAEV. Yes . . . But why are you looking at me like that?

VERA [*to herself*]. Ah, I understand! Yes, yes, she is still hoping . . .

[*The door from the corridor briskly opens. Enter Natalya Petrovna. She stops on seeing Vera and Belyaev.*]

BELYAEV. What are you saying?

VERA. Yes, it's all clear to me now. She's had second thoughts, she's realized I'm no danger to her! And really what am I—just a silly girl, while she's . . .

BELYAEV. Vera Aleksandrovna, how can you think . . .

VERA. And when all's said and done, who knows? Perhaps she's right, perhaps you are in love with her . . .

BELYAEV. Me?

VERA [*standing up*]. Yes, you. Why are you blushing?

BELYAEV. Me, Vera Aleksandrovna?

VERA. Do you love her, could you fall in love with her? Why don't you answer?

BELYAEV. But for heaven's sake what do you want me to say? Vera Aleksandrovna, you're so excited! Calm down, for God's sake!

VERA [*turning away from him*]. Oh, you're treating me like a child! You don't even have the decency to give me a serious answer. You simply want to be rid of me ... you're humouring me! [*She is about to leave, but suddenly stops at the sight of Natalya Petrovna.*] Natalya Petrovna! [*Belyaev swiftly glances round.*]

NATALYA PETROVNA [*taking a few steps forward*]. Yes, it's me. [*She speaks with a certain effort.*] I came to find you, Verochka.

VERA [*slowly and coldly*]. What made you come here precisely? You were looking for me, were you?

NATALYA PETROVNA. Yes, I was looking for you. You're not careful enough, Verochka ... I've mentioned this to you before. And you, Aleksei Nikolaich, you've forgotten your promise, you've deceived me.

VERA. Natalya Petrovna, that's enough, stop! [*Natalya Petrovna looks at her in astonishment.*] I've had enough of you talking to me like a child. [*Lowering her voice:*] From today on I'm a woman—I'm a woman like you!

NATALYA PETROVNA [*in confusion*]. Vera ...

VERA [*almost in a whisper*]. He hasn't deceived you. It wasn't he who wanted this meeting. After all, he doesn't love me, you know that and you've no need to be jealous.

NATALYA PETROVNA [*with increasing astonishment*]. Vera!

VERA. Believe me, you don't have to pretend any more. Being sly won't help now. I can see through it now ... Believe me, Natalya Petrovna, I'm no longer your ward whom you look after [*Ironically.*] like an older sister ... [*Moves towards her.*] I'm your rival.

NATALYA PETROVNA. Vera, you're forgetting yourself ...

VERA. Perhaps ... but who's made me? I don't myself understand where I've got the courage from to talk to you like this ... Perhaps I'm talking like this because I've got nothing more to hope for, because you tried to trample all my feelings underfoot—and you've succeeded

... completely! But please listen: I don't intend to pretend to you as you did to me. You'd better know that ... [*Pointing at Belyaev.*] I've told him everything.

NATALYA PETROVNA. What could you have told him?

VERA. What could I? [*With irony.*] Everything I managed to notice. You hoped you'd get everything out of me without giving yourself away. You were wrong, Natalya Petrovna. You were much too sure of yourself ...

NATALYA PETROVNA. Vera, Vera, take care ...

VERA [*in a whisper and approaching even closer to her*]. Tell me I'm wrong! Tell me you don't love him! He told me he didn't love me! [*Natalya Petrovna is silent and embarrassed. Vera stands still and suddenly places her hand on her forehead.*] Natalya Petrovna, forgive me ... I ... I myself don't know ... what's happened to me. Forgive me, don't be hard on me ...

> [*She bursts into tears and exits hastily through the door into the corridor. There is silence.*]

BELYAEV [*approaching Natalya Petrovna*]. I can assure you, Natalya Petrovna ...

NATALYA PETROVNA [*staring motionlessly at the floor and stretching a hand out in his direction*]. Stop, Aleksei Nikolaich. It's true. Vera's right, it's time ... it's time for me to stop pretending. I'm guilty before her, before you—and you have every right to despise me. [*Belyaev makes an involuntary gesture.*] I've debased myself in my own eyes. I've only got one way of earning your respect again—to be frank, completely frank, no matter what the consequences are. In any case, I am seeing you for the last time and I am speaking to you for the last time. I *am* in love with you. [*She still does not look at him.*]

BELYAEV. You, Natalya Petrovna!

NATALYA PETROVNA. Yes, me. I *am* in love with you. Vera wasn't mistaken and didn't mislead you. I fell in love with you the day you arrived, but I didn't admit it to myself until yesterday. I have no intention of justifying my conduct . . . It was unworthy of me. But at least now you can understand and forgive. Yes, I was jealous of Vera. Yes, I thought of marrying her off to Bolshintsov, so as to put her out of reach of me and you. Yes, I made use of my superiority in age and position to worm her secret out of her and, of course, I hadn't expected it and I gave myself away. I *am* in love with you, Belyaev. But you must realize it's only pride that makes me admit it . . . The comedy I've been playing out until now has finally disgusted me. You can't stay here any longer . . . However, after what I've just said to you, you'll probably feel extremely embarrassed in my presence and will want to leave as soon as possible. I'm certain about that. This certainty has given me courage. I confess I wouldn't want you to take away with you unpleasant memories of me. You know everything now . . . Perhaps I spoiled things for you, perhaps if this hadn't happened you'd have fallen in love with Verochka . . . I've only got one excuse, Aleksei Nikolaich: it was all beyond my control.

[*She falls silent. She has said all this in a fairly level and calm voice, without looking at Belyaev. He has said nothing. She continues with a certain excitement, still not looking at him.*]

Can't you say something? Still, I understand. There's nothing left for you to say. The position of someone who is not in love and has a confession of love made to him is altogether too painful. I thank you for your silence. Believe me, when I said I was in love with you I wasn't pretending . . . as I had been. I wasn't counting on anything. On the contrary, I wanted to tear from myself the mask which, I can assure you, I'd never got used to . . . And anyhow there's no point in putting on a great show when everything's out in the open. What's the point of pretending when there's no one there to be fooled? Everything's now over between us. I won't keep you any longer. You can go away from here without saying a word to me, without even saying goodbye. I not only won't consider that impolite, on the contrary I'll be grateful to you. There are times when delicacy is inappropriate—even worse than rudeness. Evidently we weren't intended to get to know one another. Goodbye. Yes, we weren't intended to get to know one another . . . But at least I hope that I've now ceased to be in your eyes the oppressive, secretive and sly creature I was . . . Goodbye, for ever. [*Belyaev, in his excitement, tries to say something and cannot.*] Why aren't you going?

BELYAEV [*bows, makes as if to go and after a certain struggle with himself returns*]. No, I can't go . . . [*Natalya Petrovna looks at him for the first time.*] I can't go just like this! Look, Natalya Petrovna, you've just told me . . . you wouldn't want me to take away with me unpleasant memories of you, but I also wouldn't want you to remember me as a man who . . . My God, I don't know how to put it! . . . Natalya Petrovna, forgive me, I don't know how to talk to ladies. Until now I've only known . . . a completely different sort of woman. You say we weren't intended to get to know one another, but, I ask you, could I, a simple, almost uneducated boy, even so much as think of having a relationship with you? Think who you are and who I am! Think a moment, could I dare to imagine me . . . and someone with your background? I mean background, so just look at me—this old coat of mine and your perfumed dresses! I ask you! Yes, of course I was frightened of you and I'm frightened now! Without any exaggeration I looked up to you as a higher being and now you say . . . you say you're in love with me, you, Natalya Petrovna, in love with *me*! I feel my heart beating inside me as it's never beaten before in my entire life and it's not just out of astonishment, it's not that I'm flattered—it's got nothing to do with feeling like that! But I can't just go! It doesn't matter what you say!

NATALYA PETROVNA [*after a pause, as if to herself*]. My God, what have I done!

BELYAEV. Natalya Petrovna, in God's name, believe me . . .

NATALYA PETROVNA [*in a changed voice*]. Aleksei Nikolaich, if I didn't know you were a man of honour,
someone devoid of falsehood, I could have God knows
what thoughts now! Perhaps I would regret my frankness. But I believe you. I don't want to hide my feelings
from you and I tell you I am grateful to you for what
you've just said. I know now why we didn't become
friends . . . It wasn't anything about me personally that
put you off, it was only my position . . . [*Stops.*] All's for
the best, of course, but it'll be easier now for me to say
goodbye . . . Goodbye. [*Is on the point of leaving.*]

BELYAEV [*after a pause*]. Natalya Petrovna, I know I can't
stay here, but . . . but I can't tell you everything that's
happening inside me. You're in love with me . . . it's
terrible for me even to say the words, it's all so new to
me! I think I'm seeing and hearing you for the very first
time, but I feel only one thing—that I must go, I feel I
can't be responsible for what may . . .

NATALYA PETROVNA [*in a weak voice*]. Yes, Belyaev, you
must go. Now, after being so frank, you can go . . . I
mean, despite everything I've done, maybe it could be
possible . . . Oh, believe me, if I could only have had an
inkling of everything you've just said, what I've confessed, Belyaev, would have died inside me . . . I simply
wanted to put an end to any misunderstandings, I
wanted to be penitent, to punish myself, I wanted to cut
the final link at one stroke. If I'd had any idea . . . [*She
covers her face.*]

BELYAEV. I believe you, Natalya Petrovna, I believe you.
I myself, just a quarter of an hour ago—could I have
imagined, after all . . . It was only today, during our
meeting before lunch, that I felt for the first time
something extraordinary, something unforeseen happening to me, like a hand squeezing my heart, and I grew all
hot . . . Before that I'd really kept away from you, as I
didn't even like you. But when you told me today that
Vera Aleksandrovna didn't feel indifferent . . . [*Stops.*]

NATALYA PETROVNA [*smiling unwillingly despite herself*].

Enough's enough, Belyaev, we mustn't think about that. We mustn't forget that we're talking together for the last time . . . and that tomorrow you're leaving . . .

BELYAEV. Oh, yes, I'll be leaving tomorrow! Now I've still got the chance of going away . . . and all this'll be over! You see I don't want to exaggerate—I'll be going, and that'll be that! I'll take away one memory, I'll remember for ever and ever that you were in love with me . . . How come I didn't know you till this moment? Look—look at me now! Could I really have tried to avoid looking at you? Could I really have been afraid of you?

NATALYA PETROVNA [*with a smile*]. You've only just told me you were frightened of me.

BELYAEV. I have? [*A pause.*] True, I did . . . I'm astonished at myself. I mean, how can I dare to talk to you like this! I don't know what's happened to me.

NATALYA PETROVNA. Are you sure you don't?

BELYAEV. How do you mean?

NATALYA PETROVNA. That you and me . . . [*Shudders.*] Oh, God, what am I doing! Listen, Belyaev, please help me . . . No woman has ever found herself in a situation like this. I really can't stand it any longer! Perhaps it's a good thing it's being ended now once and for all, but at least we've got to know each other . . . Give me your hand—and let's say goodbye for ever.

BELYAEV [*taking her hand*]. Natalya Petrovna, I don't know what to say . . . my heart's so full . . . God grant you . . . [*Stops and presses her hand to his lips.*] Goodbye. [*Starts to exit through the garden door.*]

NATALYA PETROVNA [*watching him go*]. Belyaev . . .

BELYAEV [*turning round*]. Natalya Petrovna . . .

NATALYA PETROVNA [*after a moment's silence, in a weak voice*]. Don't go . . .

BELYAEV. What?

NATALYA PETROVNA. Don't go! May God be our judge! [*She hides her head in her hands.*]

BELYAEV [*going quickly up to her and holding out his hands to her*]. Natalya Petrovna . . .

[*At that moment the garden door opens and Rakitin appears. He looks at the two of them a moment and then quickly approaches.*]

RAKITIN [*loudly*]. They're looking for you all over, Natalya Petrovna . . . [*Natalya Petrovna and Belyaev look round.*]

NATALYA PETROVNA [*taking her hands from her face and literally coming to herself*]. Ah, it's you. Who is looking for me? [*Belyaev gives Natalya Petrovna an embarrassed bow and is about to go.*] So you *are* going, Aleksei Nikolaich . . . Don't forget, you know what . . . [*He bows a second time and exits into the garden.*]

RAKITIN. Arkady is looking for you. I admit I hadn't expected to find you here, but I was just passing . . .

NATALYA PETROVNA [*with a smile*]. And you heard our voices. I came across Aleksei Nikolaich here . . . and we had a little talk. It seems today's a day for talks, but now we can go indoors . . . [*Makes as if to take the door into the corridor.*]

RAKITIN [*in a certain excitement*]. May I ask . . . what you've decided?

NATALYA PETROVNA [*pretending surprise*]. What I've decided? I don't understand you.

RAKITIN [*after a lengthy pause, sadly*]. In that case I understand everything.

NATALYA PETROVNA. Well, that's it, then—more mysterious hints! Well, yes, I had a talk with him and now everything is back as it should be. It was all nonsense, all a bit exaggerated . . . Everything you and I talked about, that was all so much childishness. We'd better forget about it now.

RAKITIN. I am not interrogating you, Natalya Petrovna.

NATALYA PETROVNA [*with a forced show of scattiness*]. What

on earth was it I wanted to say to you? Oh, I can't remember. It doesn't matter. Let's go. That's all over and done with.

RAKITIN [*looking at her intently*]. Yes, it's done with. How annoyed you must be now . . . for being so frank today, I mean. [*He turns away.*]

NATALYA PETROVNA. Rakitin . . . [*He again looks round at her; she apparently does not know what to say.*] You haven't yet spoken to Arkady, have you?

RAKITIN. No, I haven't . . . I haven't yet managed to think of anything to say. You realize something's got to be devised. . .

NATALYA PETROVNA. It's unbearable! What do they want from me? I'm hounded wherever I go! Oh, Rakitin, I do feel bad about you . . .

RAKITIN. Natalya Petrovna, please don't fret. What's the point? It's all in the nature of things. But it's quite obvious that Mr Belyaev is still a novice in such matters! The way he got confused and ran away! Still, with time . . . [*Rapidly and in a low voice.*]. . . you'll both learn not to show your feelings . . . [*Loudly.*] Let's go!

  [*Natalya Petrovna is on the point of going to him and then stops. At that moment the voice of Islaev is heard beyond the garden door saying: 'You say he came this way?' and immediately after enter Islaev and Shpigelsky.*]

ISLAEV. Right—and there he is! Well, well, well, and Natalya Petrovna's here, too! [*Going up to her.*] What is this, a continuation of today's heart-to-heart? Clearly it must be something important.

RAKITIN. I just came across Natalya Petrovna here . . .

ISLAEV. Came across? [*Looks round,*] What sort of a meeting place is this, do you think?

NATALYA PETROVNA. You just came here, after all . . .

ISLAEV. I just came here because . . . [*Stops.*]

NATALYA PETROVNA. Because you were looking for me?

ISLAEV [*after a pause*]. Yes, because I was looking for you. Don't you want to come back to the house? Tea's ready. It'll be dark soon.

NATALYA PETROVNA [*taking his arm*]. Let's go.

ISLAEV [*looking round*]. This vestibule could make a couple of good rooms for gardeners—or servants' quarters. What do you think, Shpigelsky?

SHPIGELSKY. Certainly.

ISLAEV. Let's go the garden way, Natasha. [*Goes towards the garden door. Throughout the entire scene he has not once glanced at Rakitin. In the doorway he half turns.*] Are you coming, gentlemen? Let's go and have some tea. [*Exits with Natalya Petrovna.*]

SHPIGELSKY [*to Rakitin*]. Come on, Mikhailo Aleksandrych, let's go. Give me your arm. Obviously you and I have always got to bring up the rear . . .

RAKITIN [*with feeling*]. Ah, Mr Doctor, let me just tell you that I'm bored sick of you . . .

SHPIGELSKY [*with a pretence of warm feeling*]. If only you knew how bored sick I am of myself, Mikhailo Aleksandrych! [*Rakitin smiles sadly.*] Let's go, let's go . . . [*Exit both through the garden door.*]

ACT FIVE

The scene is the same as in Acts One and Three. Morning.
ISLAEV *is sitting at the table and studying some papers. He suddenly stands up.*

ISLAEV. No! I definitely cannot go on working today. It's as if I've had a nail driven into my head! [*Walks about.*] I admit I hadn't expected it. I hadn't expected to be as alarmed as I am now. What's to be done? That's the question. [*Thinks and suddenly shouts.*] Matvei!

MATVEI [*entering*]. You called, sir?

ISLAEV. Get me the foreman . . . Oh, and tell the diggers down at the dam to wait until I get there. Off you go!

MATVEI. Yes, sir. [*Exits*]

ISLAEV [*going back to the table and sorting through the papers*]. Yes, that *is* the question!

ANNA SEMËNOVNA [*entering and going up to Islaev*]. Arkady, my dear . . .

ISLAEV. Ah, it's you, mother. How are you feeling?

ANNA SEMËNOVNA [*sitting down on the divan*]. I am well, thank God! [*Sighs.*] I am feeling well. [*Sighs more loudly.*] Thank God! [*Seeing that Islaev pays no attention to her, she sighs very loudly, with a slight sobbing sound.*]

ISLAEV. You're sighing so much . . . Is there something wrong?

ANNA SEMËNOVNA [*again sighing, but less loudly*]. Ah, Arkady, my dear, as if you didn't know why I am sighing!

ISLAEV. What do you mean?

ANNA SEMËNOVNA [*after a pause*]. I am your mother, my dear Arkady. Of course, you're grown up, with a mind of

your own. But I am still your mother. Your *mother*—
remember that word?

ISLAEV. Do please explain.

ANNA SEMËNOVNA. You know what I'm referring to, my
dear. Your wife, Natasha—of course, she's a beautiful
woman, and to date she's been a model of the best
behaviour . . . But she's still so young, my dear Arkady,
and youth is . . .

ISLAEV. I know what you mean. You think her relationship
with Rakitin . . .

ANNA SEMËNOVNA. God forbid! I wasn't thinking about
that at all . . .

ISLAEV. You didn't let me finish. You think that her
relationship with Rakitin is not entirely, er, entirely clear.
The mysterious talks, the tears—you think them rather
odd.

ANNA SEMËNOVNA. What, my dear Arkady, did he tell
you these talks between them were all about? He's said
nothing to me.

ISLAEV. I haven't yet questioned him about that, mother.
And he clearly hasn't been in a hurry to satisfy my
curiosity.

ANNA SEMËNOVNA. So what do you intend to do about it?

ISLAEV. I do not intend to do anything, mother.

ANNA SEMËNOVNA. What, nothing at all?

ISLAEV. Nothing at all.

ANNA SEMËNOVNA [*standing up*]. I confess that astonishes
me. Of course, you're master in your own home and
know better than me what's right and what's wrong.
However, just think of the consequences . . .

ISLAEV. Really and truly, mother, you're getting worked
up over nothing.

ANNA SEMËNOVNA. My dear, I *am* your mother! However,
you know best. [*A pause.*] I must tell you that I came to

find you with the intention of offering to be a go-between . . .

ISLAEV [*animatedly*]. No, mother, I must beg you not to worry yourself on that account . . . Please!

ANNA SEMËNOVNA. As you wish, my dear, as you wish. I won't say another word about it. I've warned you and done my duty—and now it's just water under the bridge. [*A short silence ensues.*]

ISLAEV. Aren't you going out for a drive anywhere today?

ANNA SEMËNOVNA. It's just that I must warn you—you're too trusting, my dear, you judge everyone by your own standards! Believe me, in our time real friends are all too rare!

ISLAEV [*impatiently*]. Mother, really . . .

ANNA SEMËNOVNA. Very well, I won't say a word, not a word! And who'd listen to me, just an old woman? I mean, I'm obviously out of my mind! I was taught different standards and I tried to pass them on to you . . . Well, get on with your work, I won't disturb you any more. I'll be off. [*Goes to the door and stops.*] So?. . . Well, you know best, you know best! [*Exits.*]

ISLAEV [*gazing after her*]. Why do people who genuinely love you always want to take turns sticking their fingers into your wounds? They're always so sure you'll feel better for it—that's what's so amusing! However, I'm not blaming mother. She has the very best of intentions, so why shouldn't she give me some advice? But that's not the point . . . [*Sitting down.*] What am I going to do? [*After a moment's thought, stands up.*] The simpler, the better! Diplomatic niceties don't suit me. I'm always the first one to get mixed up! [*Rings a bell. Matvei enters.*] Do you know whether Mikhailo Aleksandrych is at home?

MATVEI. He's at home, sir. I saw him a moment ago in the billiard room.

ISLAEV. Ah! Well, ask him to come and see me.

MATVEI. Yes, sir. [*Exits.*]

ISLAEV [*walking backwards and forwards*]. I'm not accustomed to these upsets. I hope they won't happen often. Although I've got a strong constitution, I can't stand this sort of thing. [*Places his hand on his heart.*] Phew!

[*Rakitin enters from the hall looking embarrassed.*]

RAKITIN. You wanted to see me?

ISLAEV. Yes . . . [*After a pause.*] Michel, you are in my debt.

RAKITIN. I am?

ISLAEV. Don't you remember? Surely you haven't forgotten your promise, have you? About Natasha's tears, I mean—and generally speaking. You remember when mother and I came across the two of you, you told me you had a secret which you wanted to explain.

RAKITIN. Did I say it was a secret?

ISLAEV. You did.

RAKITIN. What on earth sort of secret could there be between us? We had been having a talk.

ISLAEV. What about? Why was she crying?

RAKITIN. You know, Arkady, there are times even in the life of the happiest woman when . . .

ISLAEV. Rakitin, stop, that's enough! I can't bear seeing you in this state. Your embarrassment is much more worrying to me than it is to you. [*Takes him by the arm.*] We are old friends. I've known you since you were a boy. I don't know how to pretend to you—and you've always been frank with me. Let me put a question to you . . . I give you my word of honour that I won't doubt the sincerity of your answer. Are you in love with my wife? [*Rakitin looks at Islaev.*] You know what I mean: Are you in love with her . . . Well, in short, do you love my wife with the kind of love that you would find it hard to admit to her husband?

RAKITIN [*after a pause, in a hollow voice*]. Yes, I do love your wife . . . with that kind of love.

ISLAEV [*also after a pause*]. Michel, thank you for being so
frank. You're a good and noble man. However, what's to
be done now? Sit down and we'll discuss the matter
between us. [*Rakitin sits down. Islaev walks about the room.*]
I know Natasha, I know what she's worth . . . But I also
know what I'm worth. I'm not worth as much as you,
Michel—please don't interrupt me—I'm not worth as
much as you. You're cleverer, better and, finally, you're
more sociable than I am. I'm a simple man. Natasha
loves me—or so I think, but she has eyes in her head . . .
well, in short, she must be fond of you. This is what I
want to say to you: I noticed your mutual sympathy for
each other a long time ago, but I always trusted both of
you and so far nothing's come to light—oh, I'm no good
at expressing myself! [*Stops.*] But after yesterday's scene
and after your second talk last evening, what am I to
make of things? If only I alone had come across you . . .
But there were witnesses—mother and that fool Shpigelsky . . . Well, what do you say, Michel, eh?

RAKITIN. You're absolutely right, Arkady.

ISLAEV. That's beside the point. The point is—what do
we do? I must tell you, Michel, that though I'm a simple
man I understand things well enough to know it's wrong
to blight someone else's life and that there are times
when one shouldn't insist on one's own rights. This isn't
something I've picked up from books, my dear chap, it's
my own conscience speaking. Give people freedom—
what d'you say, eh? Give people freedom! Only one's got
to think things over. It's much too important.

RAKITIN [*standing up*]. I've already thought it over.

ISLAEV. What?

RAKITIN. I must leave . . . I am going.

ISLAEV [*after a pause*]. You think so? Go right away from
here?

RAKITIN. Yes.

ISLAEV [*again beginning to walk to and fro*]. That really *is* something! But perhaps you're right. We'll be at a loss without you—God knows, perhaps it won't do the trick. But you should know best, you've got a clearer picture. I presume you've thought it all out, well and truly. You're a danger to me, my dear chap . . . [*With a sad smile.*] Yes, you really are! What I said a moment ago about freedom . . . well, for heaven's sake, I'd never have lived through it! To be without Natalya would be for me like . . . [*Waves his hand.*] And there's something else: for some while, particularly recently, I've seen a great change in her. She's shown signs of experiencing a deep, on-going excitement which frightens me. I'm not wrong, am I?

RAKITIN [*bitterly*]. Oh, no, you're not wrong!

ISLAEV. Well, you see! So you'll be going, will you?

RAKITIN. Yes.

ISLAEV. Hmm. How sudden it's all been! Did you have to look quite so put out when mother and I came across you . . .

MATVEI [*entering*]. The foreman's arrived, sir.

ISLAEV. Let him wait! [*Exit Matvei.*] Michel, will you be away for long? This is all nonsense, my dear chap!

RAKITIN. I really don't know . . . I think it'll be . . . a long time.

ISLAEV. You don't take me for some kind of Othello, do you? Really, I don't think there's been a conversation like this between friends since the world began! I can't just say goodbye to you like this . . .

RAKITIN [*pressing his hand*]. You let me know when I can come back.

ISLAEV. There isn't anyone here to take your place! Certainly not Bolshintsov!

RAKITIN. There are others round here . . .

ISLAEV. Who? Krinitsyn? That fop! Belyaev's a good chap, of course . . . but you and he are worlds apart!

RAKITIN [*caustically*]. You think so? You don't know him,

Arkady . . . Just you pay him some attention. That's my advice to you, do you hear? He is a very . . . a very remarkable man.

ISLAEV. Bah! You and Natasha wanted to concern yourselves with his education! [*Glances towards the door.*] Ah, there he is, I think! He's coming this way! [*Hurriedly.*] So, my dear chap, it's all decided—you're going away, just for a short time, in a few days. There's no need for hurry—one must prepare Natasha for it . . . I'll put things right with mother . . . And may God grant you happiness! You've lifted a stone from my heart. Embrace me, my dear friend! [*Hurriedly embraces him and turns to face the incoming Belyaev.*] Ah, it's you! Well, how are things?

BELYAEV. All right, Arkady Sergeich.

ISLAEV. So where's Kolya?

BELYAEV. He is with Mr Schaaf.

ISLAEV. Splendid! [*Picks up his hat.*] Well, gentlemen, goodbye. I haven't been anywhere today, neither down at the dam, nor at the building site. You see, I've just been looking at papers. [*Tucks them under his arm.*] Goodbye! Matvei! Matvei! Come along! [*Exits.*]

    [*Rakitin remains lost in thought downstage.*]

BELYAEV [*going up to Rakitin*]. How are you today, Mikhailo Aleksandrych?

RAKITIN. Thank you very much. I feel as usual. And you?

BELYAEV. I am well.

RAKITIN. That's obvious!

BELYAEV. Why do you say that?

RAKITIN. Because I can see it—from your face. And, what's more, you've got on a new coat today! And what's that? Ah, a flower in your buttonhole! [*Belyaev, reddening, tears it out.*] Why on earth did you do that? It's very charming . . . [*After a pause.*] By the way, Aleksei Nikolaich, if you need anything, I'm going into town tomorrow.

BELYAEV. Tomorrow?

RAKITIN. Yes . . . And from there perhaps to Moscow.

BELYAEV [*in surprise*]. To Moscow? I thought you told me
yesterday that you intended to stay here about a
month . . .

RAKITIN. Yes, but matters . . . It's turned out that . . .

BELYAEV. Will you be gone for long?

RAKITIN. I don't know. It could be a long time.

BELYAEV. May I ask—does Natalya Petrovna know your
intention?

RAKITIN. No. Why do you ask particularly about her?

BELYAEV. Why? [*Slightly embarrassed.*] I just wondered . . .

RAKITIN [*after a pause and looking round him*]. Aleksei Nikolaich, I think that, apart from ourselves, there's no one
in the room, so doesn't it strike you as odd that we
should be playing out such a comedy to each other?
What do you think, eh?

BELYAEV. I don't understand you, Mikhailo
Aleksandrych.

RAKITIN. Really? You really don't know why I'm going
away?

BELYAEV. No.

RAKITIN. That's strange . . . Still, I'm prepared to believe
you. Perhaps you really don't know the reasons . . . If
you like, I'll tell you why I'm leaving?

BELYAEV. Please.

RAKITIN. You see, it's like this, Aleksei Nikolaich—I hope
you'll keep this to yourself, mind—you saw me just now
with Arkady Sergeich and we'd had a fairly important
talk. As a result of that talk I've decided to leave. Have
you any idea why? I'll tell you all about it, because I
consider you a man of honour . . . *He* had imagined that
I was, well . . . well, in love with Natalya Petrovna. What
do you make of that, eh? A strange notion, isn't it? But

I'm grateful to him that he wasn't sly about it, didn't put us under observation or anything, but simply turned straight to me. Well, now you tell me what you would have done in my place. Of course, his suspicions had no foundation, but they alarmed him. For the sake of his friends' peace of mind a decent man must know on occasion how to sacrifice his own . . . his own pleasure. That's why I'm leaving. I'm sure you'll endorse my decision, won't you? You'd have behaved in exactly the same way in my position, wouldn't you? You'd have left as well, wouldn't you?

BELYAEV [*after a pause*]. I might have.

RAKITIN. I'm very pleased to hear that. Of course, I don't dispute that my intention to withdraw from the situation has its comic side, in that I might consider myself a dangerous rival, but you see, don't you, Aleksei Nikolaich, a woman's honour is such an important thing . . . And what's more—I say this, naturally, not about Natalya Petrovna—I have known women pure and innocent at heart, absolute children despite their intellects, who, precisely because of this purity and innocence, have been more prone than others to surrender to some sudden infatuation . . . Or who knows why? Excessive caution in such circumstances is no hindrance, all the more so since . . . By the way, Aleksei Nikolaich, you still imagine, perhaps, that love is earth's greatest blessing?

BELYAEV [*coldly*]. I have not yet experienced it, but I think that to be loved by a woman whom you love must be a great happiness.

RAKITIN. God grant you keep such a pleasant conviction for a long while yet! In my opinion, Aleksei Nikolaich, any love, whether happy or unhappy, is a real disaster if you submit to it totally . . . Just hold on a moment! Perhaps you will still get to know how those tender hands can torture, with what gentle solicitude they can tear your heart to shreds . . . Just one moment! You will get to know how much torrid hatred is hidden beneath the most fiery love! You will remember me when, like a sick man yearning for health, you will thirst for peace of mind, the most senseless and most ordinary peace of mind, when you will envy anyone his chance of being unworried and free . . . No, no, just a moment! You will get to know what it means to belong to a skirt, what it means to be enslaved and infected—and how shameful and tiresome such slavery is! You will get to know in the end what silly little pleasures are bought at such a high price . . . But there's no point in my telling you all this when you won't believe me now. The fact is I'm very pleased to have your approval . . . yes, yes . . . in such circumstances one has to be careful.

BELYAEV [*who has never taken his eyes off Rakitin the entire time*]. Thank you for the lecture, Mikhailo Aleksandrych, though I didn't need it.

RAKITIN [*takes him by the hand*]. You must forgive me, please. I did not have the intention of . . . of giving anyone a lecture ever. I simply started chattering.

BELYAEV [*with a touch of irony*]. For no reason at all?

RAKITIN [*becoming a little mixed up*]. Precisely, for no particular reason. I simply wanted to . . . So far, Aleksei Nikolaich, you've not had the opportunity to study women. Women are a very wilful species.

BELYAEV. Who are you referring to?

RAKITIN. Oh, no one in particular.

BELYAEV. To all of them in general, is that it?

RAKITIN [*with a forced smile*]. Yes, perhaps. I don't really know why I've adopted this lecturing tone, but allow me in saying goodbye to give you a piece of kindly advice. [*Stops and gives a wave of the hand.*] Oh, I'm not the one to give advice! Please forgive me for speaking so freely . . .

BELYAEV. Not at all, not at all . . .

RAKITIN. So is there anything you need in town?

BELYAEV. Nothing, thank you. But I'm sorry you're leaving.

RAKITIN. My humble thanks for that. Believe me that I am also . . . [*Natalya Petrovna and Vera enter from the door into the study. Vera is very sad and pale.*] I was very glad to make your acquaintance . . . [*Again presses his hand.*]

NATALYA PETROVNA [*looking for a short while at both of them and then approaching them*]. Hello, gentlemen.

RAKITIN [*turning round hurriedly*]. Good morning, Natalya Petrovna . . . Good morning, Vera Aleksandrovna . . .

[*Belyaev bows silently to Natalya Petrovna and Vera. He is embarrassed.*]

NATALYA PETROVNA [*to Rakitin*]. What are you up to here?

RAKITIN. Oh, nothing . . .

NATALYA PETROVNA. Vera and I have been for a stroll in the garden. It's so pleasant out-of-doors today. The limes have such a sweet smell. It's lovely listening to the buzzing of the bees in the shade above one's head . . . [*Shyly, to Belyaev.*] We had hoped we might meet you. [*Belyaev says nothing.*]

RAKITIN [*to Natalya Petrovna*]. Oh, I see, today you're turning your attention to the beauties of nature! [*A short pause.*] Aleksei Nikolaich couldn't go out into the garden, he's wearing his new coat today . . .

BELYAEV [*slightly irritated*]. Of course, it's the only one I've got and in the garden it might get torn . . . Is that what you mean?

RAKITIN [*reddening*]. Oh, no—I didn't mean to . . . [*Vera walks silently to the divan on the right, sits down and picks up her embroidery. Natalya directs a forced smile at Belyaev. There is a short, fairly onerous silence. Rakitin continues in a tone of acerbic nonchalance.*] Oh, yes, I forgot to tell you, Natalya Petrovna, I'm leaving today . . .

NATALYA PETROVNA [*in some confusion*]. You're leaving? Where are you going?

RAKITIN. To town. On business.

NATALYA PETROVNA. I hope it won't be for long, will it?

RAKITIN. As long as it takes.

NATALYA PETROVNA. Make sure you come back soon. [*To Belyaev, not looking at him.*] Aleksei Nikolaich, are they your drawings Kolya was showing me? Did you do them?

BELYAEV. Yes, ma'am, I did . . . just doodles . . .

NATALYA PETROVNA. On the contrary, they're very charming. You have talent.

RAKITIN. I see that you are finding new virtues in Mr Belyaev with each day that passes.

NATALYA PETROVNA [*coldly*]. Perhaps . . . So much the better for him. [*To Belyaev.*] You probably have other drawings, you must show them me. [*Belyaev bows.*]

RAKITIN [*who has spent the whole time as if standing on needles*]. I think it's time I started packing . . . Goodbye. [*Goes towards the hall doors.*]

NATALYA PETROVNA [*in his direction*]. You will be seeing us before you go . . .

RAKITIN. Of course . . .

BELYAEV [*after some indecisiveness*]. Wait a moment, Mikhailo Aleksandrych, I'll be coming with you. There's a couple of things I want to say to you . . .

RAKITIN. Ah!

[*Both exit into the hall. Natalya Petrovna remains centre stage; after a moment she sits down on the left.*]

NATALYA PETROVNA [*after a short silence*]. Vera!

VERA [*without raising her head*]. What is it?

NATALYA PETROVNA. Vera, for God's sake, don't treat me like this . . . Please, Vera . . . Verochka . . . [*Vera says nothing. Natalya Petrovna rises, crosses the stage and drops on to her knees in front of her. Vera tries to make her get up, turns away and covers her face. Natalya Petrovna speaks in a kneeling position.*] Vera, forgive me. Don't cry, Vera. I'm the one who's wronged you, I'm the guilty one. Can't you please forgive me?

VERA [*through tears*]. Get up, please get up . . .

NATALYA PETROVNA. I won't get up, Vera, until you forgive me. It's terribly hard for you, but do you think it's any easier for me? Just consider, Vera ... after all, you know it all ... The only difference between us is that you've not wronged me, but I have ...

VERA [*bitterly*]. If only that were the only difference! No, Natalya Petrovna, there's another difference between us ... Today you're so soft, so kind, so gentle ...

NATALYA PETROVNA [*interrupting her*]. Because I know how wrong I've been ...

VERA. Really? Only because of that?

NATALYA PETROVNA [*standing up and sitting down next to her*]. What other reason can there be?

VERA. Natalya Petrovna, don't go on torturing me, don't go on asking questions ...

NATALYA PETROVNA [*sighing*]. Vera, I see you can't forgive me.

VERA. You are so kind and so gentle today because you feel that you are loved.

NATALYA PETROVNA [*in embarrassment*]. Vera!

VERA [*turning towards her*]. Well, isn't it true?

NATALYA PETROVNA [*sadly*]. You must believe me, we're both equally unhappy.

VERA. He loves you!

NATALYA PETROVNA. Vera, what's the point of torturing each other? It's time the two of us took stock. Just remember what my position is, what both our positions are. Just remember that two people here already know our secret—through my fault, of course ... [*Stops.*] Vera, instead of tearing each other apart with suspicions and reproaches, wouldn't it be better if the two of us thought about how to get out of this difficult situation and save ourselves? Do you imagine I can stand all these excitements and anxieties? Or have you forgotten who I am? But you're not listening to me ...

VERA [*looking thoughtfully at the floor*]. He loves you . . .

NATALYA PETROVNA. Vera, he is going away.

VERA [*turning away*]. Oh, leave me alone!

[*Natalya Petrovna looks at her indecisively. At that moment the voice of Islaev resounds in the study: 'Natasha, Natasha, where are you?'*]

NATALYA PETROVNA [*quickly standing up and going to the study door*]. I'm here. What do you want?

ISLAEV'S VOICE. Come in here, I've got something to say to you . . .

NATALYA PETROVNA. Coming! [*She returns to Vera and stretches out a hand to her. Vera does not respond. Natalya Petrovna sighs and exits into the study.*]

VERA [*alone, after a pause*]. He loves her! And I've got to stay here with her in this house . . . Oh, it's too much! [*She covers her face with her hands and remains motionless. Through the door leading to the hall appears Shpigelsky's head. He looks round cautiously and goes on tiptoe towards Vera, who does not notice him.*]

SHPIGELSKY [*standing in front of her, his arms crossed and a wicked smile on his face*]. Vera Aleksandrovna! Ah, Vera Aleksandrovna . . .

VERA [*raising her head*]. Who is it? Oh, it's you, doctor . . .

SHPIGELSKY. My dear young lady, are you ill, or what?

VERA. No, it's nothing.

SHPIGELSKY. Let me feel your pulse. [*Feels her pulse.*] Hmm, why's it going so fast? Oh, my dear young lady, my dear young lady, you've not been listening to me . . . But I've only wished you what's for your own good.

VERA [*glancing up at him decisively*]. Ignaty Ilich . . .

SHPIGELSKY [*briskly*]. At your service, Vera Aleksandrovna. What a look you're giving me! Yes, ma'am.

VERA. That gentleman—Mr Bolshintsov, your friend—is he really a nice man?

SHPIGELSKY. You mean my friend Bolshintsov? The most splendid, most honest man ... the very model of all that's best!

VERA. He's not a wicked man?

SHPIGELSKY. The kindest, I assure you. He's not a man, he's a piece of dough! You only need to take him and knead him. You won't find another such if you searched the whole wide world! He's a cooing dove, not a man!

VERA. You'll vouch for him?

SHPIGELSKY [placing one hand on his heart and raising the other above his head]. As I vouch for my very own self!

VERA. In that case you can tell him that ... that I'm ready to marry him.

SHPIGELSKY [in delighted astonishment]. You don't say!

VERA. Only it must be as soon as possible, do you hear? Just as soon as possible ...

SHPIGELSKY. Tomorrow, if you like ... Really, Vera Aleksandrovna, what a marvellous young lady you are! I'll rush over to him rightaway. This'll really delight him! What a turn-up! You know, he simply adores you, Vera Aleksandrovna ...

VERA [impatiently]. I wasn't asking you about that, Ignaty Ilich.

SHPIGELSKY. You know best, Vera Aleksandrovna, you know best. It's just that you'll be happy with him, you'll thank me, you'll see ... [Vera makes another impatient gesture.] Well, not a word, then. I won't say another word ... So I can tell him?

VERA. Yes you can.

SHPIGELSKY. Very good, ma'am. I'll be off at once. Until our next meeting ... [Listens.] Someone's coming. [Goes towards the study and in the doorway grimaces to himself in astonishment.] Au revoir [Exits.]

VERA [watching him go]. Just as quick as you can, so long as I don't have to stay here ... [Stands up.] Yes, I've

decided. I will not stay in this house—not for anything.
I can't stand the soppy way she looks at me, the way she
smiles, I can't bear watching how she sighs and looks all
smug in her happiness ... After all, she *is* happy, no
matter how much she tries to seem sorrowful and sad. I
can't bear the way she touches me ... [*Belyaev appears in
the hall doorway. He looks around and walks over to Vera.*]

BELYAEV [*in a low voice*]. Vera Aleksandrovna, are you
alone?

VERA [*looking round, shuddering and saying after a pause*]. Yes.

BELYAEV. I'm glad you're alone. Otherwise I wouldn't
have come here. Vera Aleksandrovna, I've come to say
goodbye to you.

VERA. To say goodbye?

BELYAEV. Yes, I'm leaving.

VERA. You're leaving? You as well?

BELYAEV. Yes ... me too. [*With strong suppressed excitement.*]
You see, Vera Aleksandrovna, I can't stay here. My
being here in any case has caused all sorts of problems.
Apart from the fact that—I myself don't know how—
I've upset you and Natalya Petrovna, I've also caused a
rupture in a long-lasting friendship. It's all because of
me that Mr Rakitin is leaving and you've had a row with
your benefactress ... It's time to put a stop to it all.
After I've gone I hope everything'll calm down again
and go back the way it was. Turning the heads of rich
ladies and young girls is not my sort of thing. You'll
forget about me and, perhaps, after a while, you'll be
surprised how all this could happen. It even surprises *me*
now. I don't want to deceive you, Vera Aleksandrovna,
I'm frightened, terrified of staying here ... I just can't
tell what'll happen ... I'm just not used to this sort of
thing, you know. I feel embarrassed, I think everyone's
looking at me ... And what's more, it'll be impossible
for me now—with the two of you ...

VERA. Oh, don't bother yourself about me! I won't be
staying here long.

BELYAEV. What do you mean?

VERA. That's my secret. I shan't be any bother to you, believe me.

BELYAEV. Well, you can see, can't you, I've got to leave? Just think—it's as if I've brought a plague into the house, everyone's leaving ... Wouldn't it be better if I was the only one to go while there's still time? I've just had a serious talk with Mr Rakitin. You can't imagine how much bitterness there was in what he said ... And he well and truly made fun of this new coat of mine! And he was right! Yes, I must leave. Believe me, Vera Aleksandrovna, I can't wait for the moment when I'll be galloping off in a cart on the main road. It feels stuffy in here, I want to be outside in the fresh air. I can't tell you how bitter it'll be and, at the same time, how easy, just like someone setting off on a long journey overseas. He's sick of leaving his friends behind, and he's frightened, but meanwhile the more the waves beat happily all around him, the more the wind blows so freshly into his face, the more his pulse beats faster no matter how heavy his heart ... Yes, I really must leave. I'll go back to Moscow, to my friends, I'll get back to work ...

VERA. You love her, don't you, Aleksei Nikolaich? You love her and yet you're leaving?

BELYAEV. That's enough, Vera Aleksandrovna, why go on about it? Can't you see it's all over? Everything. It flared up and went out like a spark. Let's say goodbye as friends. It's time. I've come to my senses. Keep well, be happy, we'll see each other some time ... I'll never forget you, Vera Aleksandrovna. I was very fond of you, believe me. [*Presses her hand and adds hurriedly.*] Please give this note to Natalya Petrovna.

VERA [*looking at him in confusion*]. A note?

BELYAEV. Yes ... I won't be able to say goodbye to her.

VERA. Are you leaving at once?

BELYAEV. At once ... I've not spoken to anyone about

this, except Mikhailo Aleksandrych. He supports me. I'll go off on foot now as far as Petrovskoe. There I'll wait for Mikhailo Aleksandrych and we'll travel on together to the town. I'll write to you from there. My luggage will be sent on. You see, it's all arranged ... However, you can read the note. It's only a couple of words.

VERA [*taking the note from him*]. You really are leaving?

BELYAEV. Yes, yes ... Give her the note and tell her ... No, don't tell her anything. What would be the point? [*Listens.*] There's someone coming. Goodbye. [*Dashes to the door, stops for a moment in the doorway and then runs off. Vera remains with the note in her hand. Enter Natalya Petrovna from the drawing-room.*]

NATALYA PETROVNA [*going up to Vera*]. Verochka ... [*Looks closely and stops.*] Is there something wrong? [*Vera silently holds out the note.*] A note? From whom?

VERA [*dully*]. Read it.

NATALYA PETROVNA. You give me the shivers. [*Reads the note and suddenly presses both hands to her face and falls into an armchair. A long silence ensues.*]

VERA [*approaching her*]. Natalya Petrovna ...

NATALYA PETROVNA [*her hands still pressed to her face*]. He's leaving! He didn't even want to say goodbye to me! Oh, but at least he said goodbye to you!

VERA [*sadly*]. He didn't love me.

NATALYA PETROVNA [*removing her hands from her face and standing up*]. But he has no right to leave like this ... I want to ... He cannot just ... Who gave him the right just to push off in such a stupid way? It shows such contempt ... I ... What made him think I wouldn't decide anything? [*Sinks back into the armchair.*] My God, my God!

VERA. Natalya Petrovna, you told me only just now that he had to leave—remember?

NATALYA PETROVNA. You're all right now ... He's going. Now you and I are equal ... [*Her voice breaks.*]

VERA. Natalya Petrovna, you told me only just now—they were your very own words—'Instead of tearing each other apart, wouldn't it be better if the two of us thought about how to get out of this difficult situation and save ourselves?' We're saved now,

NATALYA PETROVNA [*Turning away from her almost in hatred*]. Ah!

VERA. I understand you, Natalya Petrovna. Don't worry. I won't burden you with my presence much longer. It's impossible for the two of us to go on living together.

NATALYA PETROVNA [*tries to stretch out her hand to her and then drops it on her knees*]. Why do you say that, Verochka? Surely you don't want to leave me as well, do you? Yes, you're right, we're saved. It's all over. Everything's back where it was . . .

VERA [*coldly*]. Don't worry, Natalya Petrovna. [*Vera looks at her in silence. Enter Islaev from the study.*]

ISLAEV [*in a low voice to Vera, after having looked for a short while at Natalya Petrovna*]. She knows that he's leaving, doesn't she?

VERA [*in bewilderment*]. Yes . . . she knows . . .

ISLAEV [*to himself*]. Why on earth has he been so quick? [*Loudly.*] Natasha. [*Takes her by the hand. She raises her head.*] It's me, Natasha. [*She forces herself to smile.*] Are you unwell, my dear? I'd advise you to lie down, I really would.

NATALYA PETROVNA. I'm all right, Arkady. It's nothing.

ISLAEV. Still, you look pale. Really, just listen to me—you go and rest a little.

NATALYA PETROVNA. Well, all right . . . [*She tries to rise and cannot.*]

ISLAEV [*helping her*]. There, you see! [*She leans on his arm.*] Would you like me to come with you?

NATALYA PETROVNA. Oh, I'm not as weak as all that! Let's go, Vera. [*Goes towards the study. Enter Rakitin from the hall. Natalya Petrovna stops.*]

RAKITIN. I've come, Natalya Petrovna . . .

ISLAEV [*interrupting him*]. Ah, Michel—a word in your ear! [*Leads him to one side—in a low voice, irritably.*] Why've you told her everything rightaway? After all, I begged you, didn't I? Why all the hurry? I found her here in such an upset state . . .

RAKITIN [*in astonishment*]. I don't understand you.

ISLAEV. You've told Natasha you were leaving . . .

RAKITIN. Do you suppose that's why she was so upset?

ISLAEV. Sssh—she's looking at us! [*Loudly.*] Aren't you going to your room, Natasha?

NATALYA PETROVNA. Yes . . . I'm on my way . . .

RAKITIN. Goodbye, Natalya Petrovna! [*Natalya puts her hand on the door handle and says nothing.*]

ISLAEV [*placing his hand on Rakitin's shoulder*]. Natasha, you know, don't you, that he's one of the best of men . . .

NATALYA PETROVNA [*in a sudden display of feeling*]. Yes, I know—he's a splendid man, you're all splendid people . . . all, all of you . . . and yet, yet . . . [*She suddenly covers her face with her hands, pushes the door with her knee and goes out quickly. Vera follows her. Islaev sits down silently at the table and leans on his elbows.*]

RAKITIN [*looking for a short while at him and shrugging his shoulders*]. So what position am I in now? Marvellous—no other word for it! Refreshing, even! And what sort of goodbye was that after four years of loving devotion? Good, a very good one, just right for someone who talks as much as I do! Yes, and thank God it's all for the best! The time had come to end the sickly, consumptive affair. [*Loudly to Islaev.*] Well, Arkady, goodbye!

ISLAEV [*raising his head, with tears in his eyes*]. Goodbye, my dear chap . . . But it's not all that easy. I hadn't expected it, my dear fellow. It's all come right out of the blue. Well, it's an ill wind, as they say, that doesn't blow anyone any good. Thank you, I'm grateful to you—you've been a real friend!

RAKITIN [*to himself, through his teeth*]. That is too much! [*Brokenly.*] Goodbye. [*Is about to exit into the hall when Shpigelsky runs into him.*]

SHPIGELSKY. What's happened? I was told Natalya Petrovna was unwell . . .

ISLAEV [*standing up*]. Who told you?

SHPIGELSKY. A girl . . . a maid . . .

ISLAEV. No, it's nothing, doctor. I think it would be better not to disturb Natasha now . . .

SHPIGELSKY. Ah, well, excellent! [*To Rakitin.*] I hear you're going into town?

RAKITIN. Yes, on business.

SHPIGELSKY. Ah, on business!

[*At that moment Anna Semënovna, Lizaveta Bogdanovna, Kolya and Schaaf all enter simultaneously from the hall.*]

ANNA SEMËNOVNA. What is it? What is it? What's happened to Natasha?

KOLYA. What's happened to Mummy? What's wrong with her?

ISLAEV. Nothing's wrong with her. I've just seen her. Why are you so bothered?

ANNA SEMËNOVNA. For pity's sake, Arkady, we were told Natasha was unwell . . .

ISLAEV. Then you were wrong to believe it.

ANNA SEMËNOVNA. Why are you so irritable, Arkady? Our concern's quite understandable.

ISLAEV. Of course, of course . . .

RAKITIN. Well, it's time for me to go.

ANNA SEMËNOVNA. You're leaving?

RAKITIN. Yes, I'm leaving.

ANNA SEMËNOVNA [*to herself*]. Ah, well, now I understand!

KOLYA [*to Islaev*]. Daddy . . .

ISLAEV. What?

KOLYA. Why's Aleksei Nikolaich gone away?

ISLAEV. Where's he gone?

KOLYA. I don't know. He gave me a kiss, put on his cap and walked away. And now it's time for the Russian lesson.

ISLAEV. He'll probably be back in a moment . . . Anyhow, we can send for him.

RAKITIN [*in a low voice to Islaev*]. Don't send for him, Arkady. He won't be coming back. [*Anna Semënovna tries to overhear; Shpigelsky is whispering to Lizaveta Bogdanovna.*]

ISLAEV. What's that mean?

RAKITIN. He's also leaving.

ISLAEV. Leaving? Where's he going?

RAKITIN. To Moscow.

ISLAEV. To *Moscow*! Is everyone out of their minds today, is that it?

RAKITIN [*lowering his voice still further*]. Between ourselves . . . Verochka fell in love with him. Well, being a man of honour, he decided to leave. [*Islaev, spreading his arms wide, sinks into an armchair.*] Now you can understand why . . .

ISLAEV [*jumping up*]. I don't understand a thing! My head's spinning! What can one make of all this? Everyone fleeing for dear life like partridges and all because they're men of honour . . . And all at once, on one and the same day . . .

ANNA SEMËNOVNA [*sidling up*]. What are you on about? Mr Belyaev, you say . . .

ISLAEV [*shouting hysterically*]. It doesn't matter, mother! Mr Schaaf, please give Kolya his lesson now instead of Mr Belyaev! Please take him off!

SCHAAF. Yes, sir. [*Takes Kolya by the hand.*]

KOLYA. But Daddy . . .

ISLAEV [*shouting*]. Go on! Go on! [*Schaaf leads Kolya away.*]
I will see you on your way, Rakitin. I'll order a horse to
be saddled and I'll see you at the dam. But you, mother,
for God's sake don't disturb Natasha—and don't you
either, doctor! Matvei! Matvei! [*Exits in a hurry. Anna
Semënovna sits down with sad dignity. Lizaveta Bogdanovna
takes up a position behind her. Anna Semënovna raises her eyes to
the ceiling as if wishing to distance herself from everything going
on around her.*]

SHPIGELSKY [*covertly and slyly to Rakitin*]. Well, Mikhailo
Aleksandrych, would you like my new little troika of
horses to take you to the main road?

RAKITIN. Ah, so you've got your horses after all?

SHPIGELSKY [*modestly*]. I reached an agreement with Vera
Aleksandrovna . . . So, would you like me?

RAKITIN. Please! [*Bows to Anna Semënovna.*] Anna Semënovna, I have the honour . . .

ANNA SEMËNOVNA [*in her usual grand manner, without rising*].
Goodbye, Mikhailo Aleksandrych . . . I wish you a
pleasant journey . . .

RAKITIN. My humble thanks. Lizaveta Bogdanovna . . .
[*Bows to her. In response she curtsies. He exits into the hall.*]

SHPIGELSKY [*approaching to kiss Anna Semënovna's hand*].
Goodbye, Madame.

ANNA SEMËNOVNA [*less grandly, but still sternly*]. Ah, are
you going as well, doctor?

SHPIGELSKY. Yes, ma'am. Patients, you know. In any
case, you see, my presence is not needed here. [*Bows all
round, screws up his eyes slyly in the direction of Lizaveta
Bogdanovna, who answers him with a smile.*] Au revoir . . .
[*Runs out following Rakitin.*]

ANNA SEMËNOVNA [*waits for him to go and, crossing her arms,
turns slowly to Lizaveta Bogdanovna*]. What do you think
about all this, my dear, eh?

LIZAVETA BOGDANOVNA [*sighing*]. I don't know, ma'am,
what to say, Anna Semënovna.

ANNA SEMËNOVNA. You heard, didn't you? Belyaev is also leaving . . .

LIZAVETA BOGDANOVNA [*again sighing*]. Oh, Anna Semë-novna, perhaps I won't be staying here any longer. I'll be leaving, too. [*Anna Semënovna gazes at her in inexpressible astonishment. Lizaveta Bogdanovna stands in front of her, not raising her eyes.*]

EXPLANATORY NOTES

The notes given below, as well as the translation, are based on the text and notes in I. S. Turgenev, *Polnoe sobranie sochinenii i pisem*, vol. 3: *Tseny i komedii 1849–1852*, Moscow–Leningrad, 1962, supplemented by the second edition of the text and notes in I. S. Turgenev, *Sochineniya*, vol. 2: *Tseny i komedii 1843–1852*, Moscow, 1979.

2 *an interval of one day in each case*: in fact, between Acts Three and Four only a few hours pass.

3 *préférence*: a three-handed card game similar to whist played usually with a pack of 32 cards, all of those below the seven being discarded; bidding usually established trumps.

3 '*Monte-Cristo se redressa haletant*': 'Monte Cristo rose, panting'; the reference is to *The Count of Monte Cristo* (1844–5) by Alexandre Dumas *père* (1802–70).

9 *ce que vous êtes pour moi*: 'What you are for me'.

16 *Morgen, morgen . . .* : 'Tomorrow, tomorrow, only not today/Is what all lazy people say': the first lines of a poem by Christian Felix Weisse (1726–1804), first published in *Lieder für Kinder* (1766).

16 *Es ist unerhört!*: '*It is unheard of!*'

18 *Mon enfant, vous feriez bien . . .* : 'My child, you ought to put on something else for dinner.'

19 '*Why pretend?*': the words of Tatyana, heroine of *Eugene Onegin* by A. S. Pushkin (1799–1836), from her final scene with Onegin, ch. 8, stanza 47.

26 *On n'entre pas . . .* : 'One doesn't come into a room like that . . . it's not the done thing.'

27 *allez en avant avec monsieur*: 'you go on ahead with Mr Belyaev.'

29 *Das ist dumm*: 'That is stupid.'

30 *beau ténébreux*: 'morosely handsome man'.

42 *Lovelace*: the hero of *Clarissa* (1747–8), the novel by Samuel Richardson (1689–1761).

136 EXPLANATORY NOTES

44 *a warm-hearted man*: the reference is thought to be to V. G. Belinsky (1811–48), the famous literary critic, whose name could not be mentioned for censorship reasons.

45 *The Montefermeil Dairymaid*: *La Laitière de Monfermeil* (1827) by Charles Paul de Kock (1794–1871). This refers to V. G. Belinsky (see previous note) who, in dire financial straits after being expelled from Moscow University, undertook a translation of Paul de Kock's *Madeleine* (1832) which was published in 1833. Due to his poor knowledge of French, the translation became notorious for its errors.

47 *Souvent femme varie* . . . : 'Woman is often changeable', the opening words of a song sung by François I in V. Hugo's drama *Le Roi s'amuse* (1832), Act IV, sc. ii. The same quotation occurs in *The Count of Monte Cristo*, vol. 2, ch. 28.

60 *That provincial Talleyrand*: Charles Maurice Talleyrand (1754–1838), French diplomat who, through his success in remaining influential during successive administrations, became a byword for unprincipled opportunism.

81 . . . *freedom and peace of mind*: the phrase echoes a line from the famous poem by M. Yu. Lermontov (1814–41) 'Alone I go out on the road' (*Vykhozhu odin ya na dorogu*, 1841).

94 *Grandma had a little grey goat*: the ditty is from a Polish source, first recorded at the beginning of the eighteenth century.